To Deven

& every dear friend

who has entered my life

at a time most needed

& least expected

Little, Brown and Company
Hachette Book Group
1290 Avenue of the Americas, New York, NY 10104
Visit us at LBYR.com

First Edition: March 2022

Little, Brown and Company is a division of Hachette Book Group, Inc. The Little, Brown name and logo are trademarks of Hachette Book Group, Inc.

The publisher is not responsible for websites (or their content) that are not owned by the publisher.

Owl icon © Panda Vector/Shutterstock.com
Emoji icons © Cosmic_Design/Shutterstock.com

Library of Congress Cataloging-in-Publication Data
Names: Sass, A. J., author.
Title: Ellen outside the lines / A. J. Sass.
Description: First edition. | New York ; Boston : Little, Brown and Company, 2022. | Includes author's note. | Audience: Ages 8–12. | Summary: "Ellen, an autistic thirteen-year-old, navigates a new city, shifting friendships, a growing crush, and her queer and Jewish identities while on a class trip to Barcelona, Spain" —Provided by publisher.
Identifiers: LCCN 2021039588 | ISBN 9780759556270 (hardcover) | ISBN 9780759556300 (ebook)
Subjects: CYAC: Autism—Fiction. | Foreign study—Fiction. | Treasure hunt (Game)—Fiction. | Gender identity—Fiction. | Sexual orientation—Fiction. | Friendship—Fiction. | Jews—Fiction. | Barcelona (Spain)—Fiction. | Spain—Fiction. | LCGFT: Novels.
Classification: LCC PZ7.1.S26476 El 2022 | DDC [Fic]—dc23
LC record available at https://lccn.loc.gov/2021039588

ISBNs: 978-0-7595-5627-0 (hardcover),
978-0-7595-5630-0 (ebook)

Printed in the United States of America

LSC-C

Printing 1, 2022

ELLEN
OUTSIDE
THE
LINES

A. J. Sass

LITTLE, BROWN AND COMPANY
New York   Boston

Chapter One

I'm ahead of schedule and this is a problem.

I know there are bigger issues. Climate change is making the oceans rise. People are cutting down trees, endangering entire forests, along with thousands of animal species. But Dr. Talia says problems like those are "out of scope." I'm supposed to think of my life as an entire world of its own, to focus on the stuff within my control.

Stuff like:

1. My breath
2. My attitude
3. The words I use

A short list, but manageable, according to Dr. Talia.

It's totally manageable. Except right now, my world's

tipped on its axis because I packed too fast but not fast enough to do anything else before my best-and-only friend, Laurel, is supposed to call.

I grab a piece of paper off my desk and head over to the suitcase lying open on my bed. I've already double- and triple-checked this packing list—I even left suit-case space for souvenirs, plus changed into clothes for tonight's Shabbat service—but it's still only 4:45.

What am I going to do for the next ten minutes?

Dropping onto my bed, I pull out my phone.

El(len) Katz

I finished packing early. You can call now.

Laurel usually responds fast. But today, my phone doesn't ring. Downstairs, Mom's voice drifts up to me. It rises then falls with each musical scale. Upstairs, it's just me and my tense shoulders, a silent phone, and the *whoosh-rattle* of the rickety ceiling fan.

My eyes drift closed, fingers curling over the edge of my mattress.

I rock in time with the fan.

Forward on the *whoosh*.

Back on the *rattle*.

Over and over.

I tell myself it's a good thing I'm ahead of schedule. It

means I can do more than I thought in the time I planned out. I imagine Dr. Talia nodding, her silvery hair swaying as she takes notes on a pad of paper:

Ellen's progress—Positive attitude: Check

I look at my phone again.

4:50 p.m.

More rocking. Another silent pep talk. Everything's fine. I've got it all under control.

Eventually my shoulders relax. I feel calm again as I head over to my desk. The surface is bare except for my dot diary, a notebook filled with schedules and lists that keep my life completely organized. It's the total opposite of Abba's messy desk, with stacks of doodles and half-finished graphic novel sketches.

I stare at the sticky note on my dot diary's cover that lists my flight confirmation number, then flip to the page with today's schedule.

Laurel's entry is under my *Events* column, but it doesn't say who's supposed to call who, just that our check-in is at 4:55 p.m., twenty-four hours before our flight departs.

It's exactly 4:55 p.m. now. I'm already feeling anxious as I unlock my phone and call Laurel.

Four rings, and then . . .

"Hi and hello!" her voice chirps. "You've reached Laurel's voice mail, so . . ."

Stomach churning, I hang up. Laurel was supposed to get home from her visit with her older sister this morning, but maybe her phone's dead after the long drive. I've never understood how Laurel can go to bed without plugging it in to charge.

I switch to her home number.

"McKinley residence."

Laurel's mom has a voice that sounds like sugar, all syrupy syllables and molasses vowels.

"Hi, Mrs. McKinley."

"Ellen! How're you doing, darlin'?"

"Good." This is a lie—the truth is I'm starting to feel sick. But according to Dr. Talia, people don't know what to say if you go off-script, and I'm the same way with schedules, so I guess I get it. "Is Laurel back from Florida?"

"Yes, indeed. She and Dahlia got in a little before lunch. It was perfect timing, really, since I'd just finished making a fresh peach cobbler and..."

As Mrs. McKinley describes each course of their meal, I pull the phone away from my ear to check the time.

5:01.

What if everyone already checked in and Laurel and I don't get seats together because peaches delayed us?

The floorboards outside my room creak with the weight of approaching feet.

"Incoming, Ellen!" Abba calls from the hall.

He swings my door open and enters my room, while Mrs. McKinley keeps talking. "It's a lovely farm, just south of Atlanta. We should take you and Laurel on a day trip." A knot forms in my stomach and travels up into my chest, making its way toward my throat. "... been in their family for at least—"

"Can I talk to Laurel?" My voice rises over hers.

Abba crosses his arms. I'm not the greatest at reading body language, but this one's easy.

"I'm sorry," I tell Mrs. McKinley, swallowing hard. "It's just, we were supposed to check in for our flight seven minutes ago."

Maybe eight now.

"Well." She pauses like she's puzzled. "I'm afraid Laurel's not here right this moment, dear. She headed over to the Taylors' after lunch. Have you tried her cell phone?"

Yes, but I can't tell her that, because my throat has closed up. I also can't tell her how things were supposed to return to normal once Laurel got back from Florida. No more messed-up schedules or canceled sleepovers. No missed calls or unanswered texts, either. Just two weeks in Spain with our Spanish class, the two of us doing everything together. She promised.

Suddenly, there's too much to focus on.

Whoosh-rattle

the fan's too loud

Scritch-scritch-scritch

cypress branches scrape against my window

Lekhah dodi

Mom sings downstairs

Hebrew words swirl in my head

Too much, too much. My temples throb.

"All my girls have been such little social butterflies," Mrs. McKinley continues, totally oblivious. "First Lily on student council, then Dahlia with all those honor societies, and now Laurel and her gymnastics..."

I meet Abba's gaze for a split second. He steps forward and holds his hand out.

"Hi, Susannah? It's Natan. Seems the girls had a miscommunication."

I don't remember handing Abba my phone. He walks a slow circle around my room, his messy bun of curly brown hair bobbing. It's longer than my red-brown hair when it's loose.

He pauses at my desk, eyes drifting to the sticky note on my dot diary. "If you have Laurel's confirmation number, I can check us all in together."

I thrum my fingers against my leg, focusing on Mom's song downstairs.

Lekhah dodi, liqrat kallah, p'ne Shabbat—short tap, tap, tap with my index finger.

Neqabelah—finger fan. First index finger, then middle, ring, and pinkie against my leg.

The rhythm helps me focus and keeps me calm.

"All right, Elle-bell. You and Laurel officially have seats together tomorrow," Abba says as he hands my phone back to me. "Hakol beseder?"

I breathe in. Abba's words are clearer. Even though I was ahead of schedule and Laurel forgot about our call, things still worked out. The fan is still rattling and the tree branches still *scritch*, but they're just background sounds now. I breathe out.

"Beseder gamur." Totally fine. I tell myself it is, even if things didn't go exactly as planned.

Still, I can't help checking my notifications to see if Laurel's texted me back.

She hasn't.

"Metzuyan. I'm glad." The corners of Abba's mouth lift and the stubble on his cheeks rise with it. His voice is a mix between Mrs. McKinley's warm Southern accent and Mom's New York–brisk that never quite went away after we moved to Georgia. Israeli airy: That's what Mom calls it. "I see you're already packed for our trip. Any chance you could help me organize my suitcase before we head to temple?"

The knot in my throat finally dissolves now that I have something else to focus on. I get up to consult my dot diary. Sunset isn't until 9:01 p.m. tonight, according to my notes, but Shabbat services start earlier. I do some quick math. "We have to leave in thirty-three minutes."

"That's doable, right?"

"Yes." I grab a pen from my desk drawer and add an entry to my *Tasks* list. "All right, let's go."

I weave us around the creakiest hallway floorboards. "Barcelona's humid in June, just like Georgia, so you'll mostly need T-shirts and shorts. You should have lots of space left over for souvenirs."

"And my art supplies?"

I glance back at him. "You are very predictable."

"True." Abba grins. "But I bet you're already coming up with a packing plan, nachon?"

"Yes." I smile a little.

He's right. Predictable might be a bad thing for some people—too boring—but not for me. And since we'll be flying halfway around the world by this time tomorrow, it's best to focus on what I can control now—like helping Abba pack his art supplies before my family leaves for temple.

Chapter Two

The next afternoon, we roll to a stop in front of the McKinleys' house, where Laurel waits for us on her wraparound porch. She hugs her family goodbye as Abba carries her luggage to the trunk.

"The two Els, reunited at last," Abba says as he and Laurel get into the car. "How was Florida, Miss Laurel?"

"I adored it." Laurel adores a lot of things, since it was her favorite word for all of seventh grade. "We drove to the Gulf last weekend. It was *so* pretty."

She rubs her small cross-shaped charm between her index finger and thumb.

Some people believe you have to look into a person's eyes to know what they're feeling, but I think you can tell more from what they do with their hands. Like, I know Abba is stressed when his knuckles turn white around his tablet pen. Mom waves her hands around as she talks when she's excited, and I do my finger thrum whenever the world gets too bright, loud, or both.

When Laurel gets nervous, she fiddles with her necklace.

She turns toward me. "It was like the beach in Savannah. Remember?"

She waits for me to say something, but the words get stuck in my throat. I nod instead, a quick, jerky movement that matches the beat of a pop song playing from our car's radio.

I remember. Last summer, between sixth and seventh grade, I spent a week with the McKinleys at their vacation home on the Georgia coast. Laurel and I swam in the ocean every morning and ate lunch on the beach each afternoon. We'd make up stories about the other tourists as we ate. Things like where they were visiting from and what might happen in their lives when they went back home.

"Sounds like you had a nice trip," Mom says.

"Yes, ma'am." Laurel's strawberry-blond hair bobs on her newly tanned shoulder. "I sure did."

We merge onto the freeway, and Abba's arms appear above his seat, stretching as far as they'll reach. "I hope no one minds if I take a nap. I lost myself in some sketches last night and stayed up past my bedtime."

"That's fine." Mom turns down the music's volume. "We'll keep quiet for you, right, girls?"

"Yes." I find my voice at the same time that Laurel says the same thing.

"Chalamot paz, Abba," I add. *Sweet dreams.*

My phone buzzes. A new text from Laurel.

I skim our last few messages.

El(len) Katz

Friday

I finished packing early. You can call now.

(Laur)el McKinley

Friday

Sorry I forgot to call 🖼 ·

I was shopping with Dahlia all morning, then SA needed a packing intervention and I totally spaced

Saturday

Forgive me?? 🙏 🙏 🙏

SA stands for Sophie-Anne Taylor. We're all students at Lynnwood Preparatory School, but Sophie-Anne has her own group of friends and I don't get how Laurel fits in with them. Ever since we met in third grade, it's always been just Laurel and me: an inseparable pair of Els. I hunch my shoulders and lean forward in my seat.

El(len) Katz

I called your house yesterday when you didn't answer your cell phone. Your mom talks a lot.

Laurel giggles. My phone buzzes again.

(Laur)el McKinley

LOLOLOL I know, I live with her

The sides of my mouth twitch up, and I relax in my seat. Up front, Mom hums a Shabbat song she sang in front of our temple this morning. I try to imagine what it'll be like to spend two Shabbats halfway across the world. Except for the trip to Savannah, I've always gone to temple with Mom and Abba every week. While Mom leads our temple in song, I sit with Abba, humming along.

Abba's breaths become deep and slow. Laurel and I keep texting to make sure we don't wake him.

(Laur)el McKinley

So how much homework do you think Señor L will make us do on this trip?

El(len) Katz

The syllabus from last year was on the school website. It's lectures in the morning, then a siesta and afternoon field trips before dinner. I didn't see times listed for homework.

(Laur)el McKinley

Let me guess…you made daily schedules for the whole trip

El(len) Katz

…maybe.

(Laur)el McKinley

I glance over at Laurel, right as Abba snorts in his sleep. The corners of our mouths rise at the same time.

Mom glances back at us in the rearview mirror. "Grins must be contagious," she tells us in a loud whisper. "Now I can't stop smiling, either."

The car rolls to a stop in front of the Atlanta airport's international departures terminal. We grab our suitcases and say goodbye to Mom. My stomach swirls with nerves as she coasts away.

Inside the airport, a group of Lynnwood students clusters together in front of the security line. Some kids

13

wear blue school T-shirts with the gold Lynnwood crest across their chests, while others wear a version with our school mascot perched on top of a shirt pocket. The brown thrasher: It's not exactly regal like a lion, tiger, or eagle, but it's the Georgia state bird and can sing up to 3,000 unique song phrases. So, it's got a few things going for it.

Abba slows, then turns back to us. "Hey, Miss Laurel. How about you head over while I run something past Ellen?"

I automatically take a step toward Laurel. We're supposed to stay together on this trip.

But Laurel doesn't seem bothered. "Sure." She turns to me. "Come find me when you're done?"

"Okay...." But I keep my eyes on her until Abba starts talking.

"I've been thinking about our last family session with Dr. Talia. Do you remember what she said?"

Dr. Talia said a lot of things last week, but one thing stayed with me enough to write it in my dot diary. "She said me being autistic isn't abnormal or bad, it's unique and different."

"Absolutely." Abba nods. "And how about right before we finished the session?"

I think back. Even though it was only a week ago, my head is filled with a flight departure time and gate number, lots of new Spanish words, and our trip's itinerary. I shake my head.

"It was just a quick mention." Abba balls his hands into fists, then flexes his fingers straight before repeating the motion. Usually he does this at his desk, when he doesn't know what to draw next. "Besides school and temple, you don't get out of the house much, so you end up spending lots of time with your mother and me. Dr. Talia said this trip could be a great time to give you some space. Does that make sense?"

"No...You're a parent chaperone. It's your job to make sure students don't get lost or hurt in Barcelona—including me."

"Of course." Abba slides his hands into his shorts pockets. "What I mean is, there may be opportunities for you and your classmates to be on your own, or times when a smaller group will only have one adult chaperone."

"Small groups?" The school website didn't say *anything* about this.

Abba nods again. "I wanted to see if you'd like me to ask your Spanish teacher to assign me to a different group, if something like that happens. To give you some independence."

My stomach flips. I shake my head fast. "No. I like spending time with you."

I expect him to smile here, like he did yesterday, but Abba just presses his lips together.

"Are you sure, Elle-bell? The parent chaperones attended an orientation, so we're equipped to assist every student, no matter what. Plus, I'd still be around if you needed anything."

"I *want* to spend time with you." I'm still shaking my head. I don't notice that I've let go of my suitcase and balled my hands into fists until Abba speaks again.

"Hey, lo hashuv. It's okay."

The distress drains out of me. My fingers relax at my sides.

"Do you need a moment, metukah?" Abba asks. "There's time to stop by the bathroom if you need someplace quiet to reset."

"No. I'm fine."

"Okay." Abba hesitates, like he's not quite convinced. Finally, he reaches for his suitcase. "Let's go join your group then."

That should be that. But as we head toward my classmates, I can't help feeling like my world has started to spin off-axis again.

Chapter Three

"Mr. Katz, Ellen!"

My Spanish teacher, Señor L, waves us over as we get closer to the security line. He stands next to a woman and a kid wearing a Lynnwood T-shirt who I don't recognize.

"Please, call me Natan." As Abba reaches out to shake his hand, I steal a glance at the people beside him. Aside from a couple of Chinese American students, Lynnwood is mostly white, including our teachers. Many of my classmates' parents went to Lynnwood when they were kids, too. Their families have lived in Georgia forever. It was a big change from my elementary school back in Brooklyn. Lots of the students there had families who had moved from other places. My Brooklyn classmates and I weren't "mostly" anything.

These two people have brown skin. My eyes linger

on a tuft of dyed purple hair framing the kid's face only to dart away when Señor L says my name.

"What?"

"I just asked how you were doing," he says. "How's your summer going, Ellen?"

Why do people ask back-to-back questions that can't have the same answer?

"Good...." I take a beat to decide how to reply to his second question. But my first answer seems to satisfy him, because he switches topics.

"Wonderful. Since you're here, Ellen Katz, meet Isa Martinez. Isa will be starting at Lynnwood in the fall and is attending this trip to get acquainted with other students."

"It's *Ee-sah*, not *Eye-saw*." We all turn to look at Isa. "As in '*Wrong lever, Kronk!*' I'm Yzma-without-the-*m*."

"Shh." Mrs. Martinez places a hand on Isa's shoulder. "Sorry, Mr. Liechtenstein. Not everyone understands Isa's sense of humor."

"Well, no worries here." Señor L claps his hands together, and I try not to wince. "Feel free to call me Señor L," he tells Isa. "Liechtenstein is a bit of a mouthful."

It's a German-speaking country, too—Laurel and I always thought it was a weird last name for a Spanish teacher. It's also weird to see a Lynnwood teacher in jeans and a T-shirt instead of dress clothes, but I guess it makes sense since students aren't required to wear school uniforms on this trip.

Señor L's T-shirt has the words *¿Cómo te...?* on it, above three cartoon llamas. It's probably supposed to be a joke, but I don't see how a trio of llamas has anything to do with the Spanish question for *What is your name?* It's not even pronounced the same.

In my head, it more logically connects to what Isa just said.

"Yzma from *The Emperor's New Groove*?" I ask.

The adults go quiet, and I wonder if I interrupted them while my thoughts were hopping from Spanish verbs to Disney llamas.

Isa's fingers curl into a thumbs-up sign. "Yep. Only my family's originally from Mexico, not South America."

Abba nudges me. "That's one of our favorite movies, isn't it, Ellen?"

I nod and steal another quick look at Isa's purple strip of hair, only to realize the other side is completely shaved. Baggy jeans and a T-shirt that hangs off narrow shoulders make me think *boy*, but I've never met a boy with a name that ends in *A*.

I've never met a girl named Isa either, though.

"And I'm Nathan-without-the-*h*," Abba says. "Although most kids just call me Mr. Katz. It's nice to meet you, Isa."

"Ellen's dad is actually a parent chaperone on this

trip," Señor L tells Isa and Mrs. Martinez. "So it might be good to talk to you both for a moment about Isa's... unique circumstances."

"Sure." Abba's voice is smooth, unconcerned. "How about you go meet up with your friends, metukah? I'll catch up soon."

Part of me wants to stay and learn about Isa's "unique circumstances," but I head off, weaving through the rest of the crowd. I pass my classmate Andy Zhang, chatting with his best friend, Noah-James Gibson, then Emmaline Delfina and Clara Bryant. I make my way up to Laurel, plus Sophie-Anne, who stands beside her.

"Hi, Ellen," Sophie-Anne says.

"Hey." I try to catch her eye, but the lights seem too bright, the floors too shiny. My gaze doesn't make it past the dark brown hair that sways halfway down her back. Laurel's told me a few times how much she *adores* Sophie-Anne's complexion. Smooth skin, no pimples in sight, or freckles that dot her face like they do mine.

"Who was that?" Sophie-Anne points.

I follow the line of her finger. "New student. Yzma-without-the-*m*."

Sophie-Anne tilts her head. "Who without the what?"

"Sophieeee! Laurel!"

Both girls twirl around. Sophie-Anne rises onto her

strappy-sandaled toes, then waves toward a check-in counter in the distance. "Madison!"

Tall, blond-haired Madison West waves back in her Lynnwood cheerleading squad tank top that says *Thrash 'em!* Her tall, blond mom stands behind her.

"I haven't seen her in, like, a month—not since her parents got divorced." Sophie-Anne turns to Laurel. "Save my spot?"

As Sophie-Anne heads toward Madison, Laurel moves closer to me. "What did your dad want to talk to you about?"

My eyes roam the security line. Classmates chatter nearby. A toddler's shriek makes my shoulders tense. I shrug, a tight up and down.

I sway a little, arms rising.

Laurel's hand catches one of mine, a silent reminder that stuff like rocking and covering my ears leads to weird looks and pointed fingers.

I drop my arms to my side, repeating Laurel's question in my head until the words start to make sense.

"Abba told me he could give me space, if I want it."

"Space?"

"He said he could keep his distance on the trip if I want more independence."

"Oh, I get it—"

"But I said no."

"Okay." Laurel twines her fingers into mine. "Well, your dad is cool, so it makes sense he'd ask. My parents never get that I don't want them around constantly."

"Lynnwood students!" Señor L's voice carries to us. "Passports out. Let's get moving."

I look past Laurel, past Sophie-Anne and Madison who are arm in arm, half walking, half skipping back to us. Abba shrugs his messenger bag up on his shoulder while Mrs. Martinez pulls Isa into a goodbye hug.

I flip through my passport to the glossy page with my picture. Laurel bounces on her toes as we roll our suitcases toward security.

"It's finally happening! Are you ready?"

She doesn't wait for me to respond, which is good because I'm not completely sure yet. When it's my turn to hand over my passport, I shuffle forward, eyes down.

There's no turning back now.

We find our gate once everyone makes it through security. Laurel reaches for my hand again, pulling me toward a pair of open seats. Our classmates spread out around us.

I open my backpack and pull out my dot diary. Every

page has a daily schedule and a task list with boxes to the left of each item. I add a checkmark when I complete a task, an *X* when an event gets canceled, and a ➔ to remind me to move something I didn't finish to the next day.

"Listen up, everyone," Señor L says before I can check off a single box.

Around me, my classmates keep talking or looking at their phones. Across from me, Isa watches Señor L, then tucks a strand of hair behind one ear, revealing a small headphone. Maybe not listening after all.

"Hey," Señor L calls, "who all's interested in grabbing snacks before the flight?"

Heads shoot up.

"Great." He smiles. "I've just got a few announcements. First, I'd like to introduce the adult chaperones. Y'all already know me from school, of course. Then there's Ellen's dad, Mr. Katz"—he gestures toward Abba—"and Emmaline's and Madison's moms, Mrs. Delfina and Mrs. West.

"Next up, we have a new student joining us: Isa Martinez." Heads swivel toward my row. "I expect everyone to be kind and give Isa a nice Lynnwood welcome."

He pauses until a few people say "Hi, Isa," including Laurel. "Perfect. Now, let's talk expectations about behavior on this flight...."

"Is that a boy or a girl?" a voice asks behind me.

I twist around and spot Noah-James Gibson at the exact moment Andy Zhang elbows him.

"Hey!" Noah-James yelps.

Señor L raises an eyebrow. "Is there a problem, boys?"

"No, sir," they say together. Señor L stares at them for a few uncomfortable seconds, then returns to his lecture.

I can't help picking up the whispers behind me.

"What'd you go and do that for?" Noah-James asks.

"You were being mean," Andy whispers back.

"I wasn't. I just want to know: boy or girl?"

"Neither." The voice is quiet but clear. My eyes dart from Señor L over to Isa, but Isa looks past me. Nearby, Señor L is rambling on about appropriate in-flight movie options and consequences for horsing around in airplane aisles.

Isa's gaze shifts and for a split second we're looking right at each other. I drop my eyes fast.

"And it's not like I've never heard that one before." Isa's lips turn up at the corners just slightly, as though Noah-James said something almost-but-not-quite funny.

Behind me, Noah-James and Andy don't utter a word.

"Now, with the ground rules for a safe and enjoyable flight clearly established, let's talk about the structure of this trip." My gaze dips down to my diary. "This should come as a pleasant surprise to anyone concerned they'd be cooped up getting lectured every morning, then herded along on afternoon field trips."

I sit up straighter.

"Studying abroad is about more than learning the same old way we do in a regular classroom. It's about experiencing a new culture and seeing sites firsthand."

Now he has my full attention.

"I'm happy to say that this year will be different, because you'll all be participating in a—drumroll, please..." Señor L waits, but no one moves. With a slight shake of his head, he continues. "Okay, fine. A scavenger hunt."

What?

The noise level ticks up as my classmates throw out questions.

"Like, we'll be searching for treasure?" Cody Mack asks.

"What's the prize?" Noah-James calls.

"I'm glad to see this level of enthusiasm." Señor L smiles. "I'll share more details once we're settled at the hotel."

I look down at my diary again, chewing on the inside of my cheek until it stings. It feels like I did all this work for nothing. I wrote out two weeks of daily schedules that are worthless now. Plus, a scavenger hunt means lots of twists and turns, wrong paths and dead ends. There are so many unknowns I can't plan out in advance.

"For now," Señor L continues, "how about we go grab some snacks?"

Laurel stands, and I copy her automatically. Around me, my classmates ask more questions, but I can't process their words. A few rows over, Abba stands, too. He smiles, but his shoulders look tense and his hands stay deep in his pockets. It reminds me of how he looked when we got to the airport earlier, when he said all those things about giving me space.

The thought pops into my head suddenly.

Abba knew. He knew about this new trip itinerary, and he didn't tell me.

Chapter Four

On the plane, Laurel takes her aisle seat and Abba his window, with me in the middle.

Laurel and I swap snack bags while the flight attendants run through safety instructions.

"Okay, Elle." Laurel points to a man in a business suit in the center row of seats.

That's my cue.

I lean toward her, trying to get a better view. "A CEO."

"You think?" Laurel's brows scrunch up. "Why isn't he in first class then?"

I consider this. "Maybe he was in Atlanta to get a loan for his business or something but the bank said no."

"*Ooh.* Good one." Laurel pops a gummy bear into her mouth. "And now he's got to go back to Spain and tell his wife the bad news."

"Yes." I've never liked when our stories have sad endings. "*Except* what he doesn't know is his wife just won the Spanish lottery. So he's going to be very happy when we land."

Laurel grins. "Perfect."

It's easy to feel like it's just Laurel and me when we make up our stories, even if Madison and Sophie-Anne are only a few rows in front of us, sitting beside Andy.

Once we've taken off, Laurel looks over at Abba. "Did you know about the scavenger hunt, Mr. Katz?"

Abba folds his hands into his lap. "Your teacher told us parents during one of the informational sessions, but he wanted it to be a surprise for the students."

Then Abba did know. A lump forms in my throat.

"So there'll be clues?" Laurel asks. "Or places we have to find on our own?"

"It wouldn't be an even playing field if I revealed anything your classmates don't know."

"No, but still!" Laurel flops back in her seat, all dramatic. As Abba pulls a magazine out of his seat pocket, she pops another gummy bear into her mouth and leans closer to me.

"You said you found last year's syllabus online, right?"

"Yes. But I don't think we'll be doing anything on it anymore."

"But *maybe* it can still give us clues about what they'll want us to look for."

I shrug.

"You wrote down all the topics that we were supposed to be learning in your notebook, right?" Laurel tries again.

I give her a stiff nod, because I did more than write them down. I looked up pictures online, printed them out, and spent hours arranging them in my dot diary's margins to match each day's agenda. La Sagrada Família. Picasso paintings. A row of stone columns in front of the National Art Museum.

"Okay, awesome," Laurel says. "Maybe we can read through your notes and get ideas."

"Before you girls get too involved in this," Abba cuts in, "there's something I want to give to Ellen."

He pulls a case out of his messenger bag and unzips it.

"Try them on," he says. "I figured they might come in handy on our flights, plus whenever you need some quiet time."

I look at the matte black noise-canceling headphones, eyes widening. Abba wears them while sketching after dinner each weeknight while Mom sings and I fill out entries in my diary. I slide them onto my ears, then Abba reaches up and clicks a button on the side of the headphones.

Battery one-hundred percent, a robotic voice says. *Connected to Ellen's iPhone.*

Then silence, like I'm underwater. The heavy drone of plane engines fades. Laurel's mouth opens and closes, but I hear almost nothing. I slide them down to my shoulders and look at Abba. "But they're yours."

"I've got my earbuds for this trip, and I'll get myself a new pair when I wrap up my next work project. These belong to you now—if you want them."

He looks at me, and it's almost like he's holding his breath. Any hint of betrayal I still feel about the change to our trip schedule dissolves fast.

"Yes." I give him a quick nod. "Todah rabah, Abba."

"You're very welcome, metukah."

As two flight attendants roll a big metal trolley past us to the front of the cabin, Laurel leans forward and digs through her bag. She sits up, showing me her own headphones. They're the same brand, but a lighter, brushed silver.

"We can pair both sets and listen to the same playlist. Look." She pulls out her phone and taps into an app.

I lean over as Laurel scrolls through a list of available devices.

"Which one is yours, Elle?"

"Probably Sheli." I check the devices list on my own

phone. There's only one flower-related Bluetooth connection that appears. "You're Bloom?"

"Yeah!"

Laurel taps on her screen and pairs us up. "What's *sheli* mean?"

"Mine," I tell her.

Beside me, Abba looks thoughtful. "Although now that it's Ellen's, maybe I should've changed it to *Shelach*, which means—"

"—yours," I finish.

"I adore that," Laurel tells me. "It's like you and your dad have a secret language. Not like with Spanish since everyone in our class studies it."

I adore it, too. Even at our temple, most people only learn Biblical Hebrew, which is different from the language people speak in Israel. Abba, Mom, and I know Modern Hebrew, so we can talk about anything we want.

"Okay, done." Laurel's voice pulls me out of my thoughts. "Put them on again."

A few beats after the music starts, I move one speaker away from my ear. "This is that song from last winter."

"Um, yeah! This is our sleepover playlist."

I pass a meal to Abba, then take mine from the flight attendant. My family keeps kosher, following kashrut rules about what food we can and can't eat and how it should be prepared. Both of our meal containers have a sticker on them that says KOSHER, so we know the food is okay to eat.

I steal a quick glance at Laurel. She doesn't seem bothered that it's been months since our last sleepover. Just thinking about it makes my skin prickle. I put my new headphones back on.

The song's melody flows through me. I let myself flap my hands in time with the music underneath my table, and my whole body relaxes.

After dinner, the cabin lights dim. The playlist has moved on to a song Laurel and I first heard while watching an online video about the physics behind gymnastics elements. I lean back and close my eyes, imagining an army of Laurels performing handsprings as I drift off to sleep.

It's only Laurel and me in my dream.

My eyes flutter open. For a moment, everything's a little dark and a lot silent. I rub my eyes, then blink. Abba comes into focus, asleep in his window seat.

My headphones are silent. I twist in my seat to check if Laurel's also asleep, then freeze.

"Hey, you're awake." Andy's voice sounds muffled

through my headphones. He tugs on the cord attached to his earbuds, and they tumble into his lap. "What's up?"

I nudge my headphones off with the back of one hand. "Where's Laurel?"

"Oh, um." Andy runs a hand through his black hair, then points up the aisle. "Just up there."

I unbuckle my seatbelt and stand, spotting the silvery strip of Laurel's headphone band. Next to her, Sophie-Anne wears matching headphones. I drop back into my seat, wondering if Laurel's sharing our playlist with Sophie-Anne.

"Laurel and I traded seats," Andy says, even though I didn't ask. "Gibs passed out just like you, and Madison still won't talk to me after..." He shrugs. "It just wasn't fun having to sit by her, but my parents checked me in late, so yeah."

It takes me a second to realize Gibs must be a nickname for Noah-James. My eyes dart to Andy's Lynnwood basketball T-shirt, with *THRASHERS PRIDE!* spelled out in bold capital letters. His hands lie clasped in his lap.

I tilt my head. "Why is Madison—"

"What's the new kid like?" Andy pauses. "Sorry. Go ahead."

"I wanted to know why Madison's not talking to you."

"Well..." Andy looks at his hands like they might hold the answer. "I kind of broke up with her."

"'*Kind of*'?" You can "kind of" understand a language you're still trying to learn, but I'm not sure how you can "kind of" break up with someone.

"Yeah," Andy says. "On the last day of school."

"Okay."

When I don't say anything else, Andy wrings his hands.

"Don't you want to know why?" he asks.

"Why what?"

"Why I broke up with her."

"No." I wanted to know why she wouldn't talk to him, so that's what I asked.

"Then you'd be the first. So, the new kid..."

"Isa Martinez," I say.

"Yeah, what's up with her? Or is it him? And why did Isa say 'neither' when Gibs asked, do you know?"

Okay, that's *way* too many questions.

"How would I know?"

Andy's brows pinch above his nose. "I just saw you talking with Isa and Señor L at the airport, so..."

He trails off as Abba stirs. Abba yawns then looks over at us. "You're not Laurel."

"No, sir."

Abba glances at me, then back at Andy.

"I changed seats with Laurel," Andy explains, "but I can ask to switch back."

"It's fine." My heart sinks as Abba extends his hand. "I'm Natan Katz, Ellen's dad."

"I know." Andy lights up. *Fisher's Final* is *incredible*. The illustrations. That plot. I've read it like ten times and still can't figure out how you did the—" He catches himself, then reaches past me to shake Abba's hand. "Sorry, I'm just a huge fan here. I'm Andy Zhang. Ellen and I had English and science together last year."

I stare at him. I didn't realize someone like Andy—popular and an athlete—noticed me enough to know which classes we had together.

"Nice to meet you." Abba smiles. "Want a sneak peek at what I'm working on next?"

"Seriously?" Andy's eyes shine under his overhead light.

"Seriously." Abba pulls out his iPad. Rainbow flag stickers in a spectrum of bright stripes decorate the cover, souvenirs he brought back from a comic convention.

He offers it to Andy. I press back into my seat as Andy leans over to take it.

"Your dad is so cool," he whispers to me.

Even though it's not too loud or too bright on this plane, something feels like it's building inside me.

"Ellen's already seen most of this stuff," Abba starts,

35

but I stand up fast. If I were as tall as Andy, I'd have hit my head on the overhead bin.

"I"—I force the words out of my tight throat—"have to use the bathroom."

"Oh, okay." Andy unbuckles his seatbelt.

I slip past him before he can stand, heading toward the lavatories at the center of the plane. Then I spot Laurel with Sophie-Anne and Madison. Turning fast, I rush to the very back.

I slip into a bathroom stall and sit on the closed toilet seat, letting myself rock.

Once. Twice.

I count from uno to sesenta.

This trip will be different than I imagined, in so many ways I can't control. The scavenger hunt is one example, but it's not the only thing that's off. It also feels like Laurel and I are growing further apart by the second.

Chapter Five

Day 1

"Señoras y señores, bienvenidos a Barcelona...."

Beside me, Laurel rubs her eyes, then fusses with her hair, even though it looks fine. "Oh my actual gosh. This flight took forever."

Nine hours, forty minutes. It's technically Sunday afternoon, but it feels like the crack of dawn, like I should still be asleep.

I didn't know what to say when Laurel returned to her seat. Even the music on our new playlist didn't help. Soon, she fell asleep. Eventually, Abba drifted off again, too.

Not me.

I say a silent goodbye to the lottery-winning CEO as we file off the plane. Señor L makes us wait until the other passengers get their suitcases from baggage claim before we can grab our own. It feels like it takes twice as long as it should, but I'm probably just tired. My body feels stiff after sitting upright for so long.

"We'll be taking a bus from here to our hotel," Señor L explains as we head outside.

I relax a little. We're back to following last year's schedule. Maybe Laurel was right. Maybe the scavenger hunt is just last year's trip in a slightly different form.

"Hoo-wee." Mrs. West fans herself. "It's hot as Hades."

Beside her, Madison rolls her eyes.

"It feels like we're walking through soup," Abba joins in.

I shift my bag up on my shoulders and my shirt sticks to my back, hot and damp. The bus driver takes our suitcases, then I follow Laurel into the passenger area. Cold, crisp air blows from ceiling vents. I breathe in deeply, grateful to be out of the heat.

"Window or aisle?" Laurel asks. Happiness tingles in my chest as I pick the window seat. Sophie-Anne and Madison take the row in front of us, and the feeling dims a little.

Then, we're off. We leave the airport behind and merge onto a freeway.

Sophie-Anne presses her face to the window. I blink the light out of my eyes, eager to see the city, too.

But everything's bright and blurry as we speed past signs, then buildings. I reach for my phone and click record. This way, I can play it back later and won't miss anything.

"Do you know if our hotel is the same one they used last year?" Laurel asks.

I nod. "It's called Hotel El Búho."

"You really do have everything memorized." Laurel laughs. "Doesn't *búho* mean 'bird'?"

"Owl."

A few minutes later, we enter a roundabout. "Passeig de Sant Joan," the driver announces. "Hotel El Búho."

Out on the sidewalk, we're reunited with our suitcases— and the humidity.

My classmates look around, chins tilting up to take everything in. I steal a quick glance up, too, before looking back at my feet. Horns honk and I catch bits of Spanish as people pass by us.

Sounds. Light. The heat. It's a lot for me to process all at once.

"This way," Señor L calls.

Eyes still down, I turn and almost collide with Laurel. One hand shades her eyes as she points toward a building. An enormous owl stares down at us with round yellow eyes.

"It's like a vintage cutout," Laurel says. "Except, what's it supposed to advertise?"

"Maybe it's like the Big Chicken," I say, imagining

39

the fifty-foot landmark that rises above a restaurant back home. "People here might use it the same way."

"Like, 'to get to the airport, take a left past El Búho and keep driving for five miles'?"

I nod, then reach for my phone to take another video.

"Elle-bell! Laurel!" We both look over at Abba, who's waving at us with one hand, holding open a door with the other.

"Well, now we know how our hotel got its name!" Laurel takes my hand.

I keep my eyes on the owl until it's out of view. Then Abba, Laurel, and I enter a foyer, where the rest of our group waits. Laurel weaves us around some of our classmates, stopping beside Sophie-Anne and Madison.

Señor L lifts a clipboard over his head. "Okay, folks. Room assignments. The boys'll be on the third floor with Mr. Katz and me, girls on the second with Mrs. West and Mrs. Delfina. There's no elevator, so let a chaperone know if you need help with your luggage." He passes a sheet of paper to Mrs. West, then heads for the stairs.

"See you soon," Abba calls as he rolls his bag toward Señor L. The boys file up the stairs first. Noah-James doesn't bother lifting his suitcase. It bangs against each step.

"That means we're actually on the third floor," Madison tells us, "because people in Europe count the ground level as floor zero."

"At least we don't have to go all the way up to the fourth floor like the boys," says Sophie-Anne as she lugs her suitcase up the steps.

Laurel and I go last. On the landing halfway up to our floor, I turn back to Laurel. "This would be easier if we were owls."

"*So* much easier."

"All right," Mrs. West calls when we all make it up to the second-floor-that's-really-the-third. "Everyone should already know who you'll be rooming with from earlier school correspondence." Smiling, Laurel catches my eye. "When I read off your room assignments, come get a set of keys. There'll be two room keys and one to get in and out of the hotel.

"First up: Clara Bryant and Emmaline Delfina are in 2A."

Clara and Emmaline step forward to get their keys. While Mrs. West hands over the 2B keys to Sully and Tess, my gaze snags on Isa hovering near the stairs, apart from the rest of us. I do some quick math. Eight girls and eight boys originally signed up for this trip, a neat, even number of two kids per room.

But now there's Isa.

"Ellen Katz and Laurel McKinley in 2C," Mrs. West continues. "And last but not least, Sophie-Anne Taylor and my little Maddie in 2D."

"For real, Mom?" Madison says under her breath.

Abba once told me I notice things on my own schedule, sometimes fast and sometimes gradual. Right now, my gaze moves beyond Laurel. Past Sophie-Anne and Madison.

"Now, settle in," Mrs. West calls as she heads down the hall. "I'll come get everyone for dinner in about ten min—"

"What about Isa?" I interrupt.

Mrs. West turns back to us. "I beg your pardon?"

Everyone's looking.

My words take off in the opposite direction, like they always do when I'm the center of attention. I'm about to shake my head when Laurel speaks up.

"You forgot a name, ma'am. Señor L said Isa Martinez is a new student."

"Ah, yes. Of course." Mrs. West looks back at the list, then over at Isa. "I'll sort this out with your teacher now, Miss Martinez."

A look passes across Isa's face that reminds me of the expression Mom makes when she hits the wrong song note. It's gone in a blink.

"I'll wait," Isa says. "No big."

"Come on, Sophie." Madison jangles the keys.

As Laurel slides a key into our door, I glance back again, but Isa's eyes are on the floor.

We enter our room, leaving Isa in the hallway. Our

room has white walls with flowery lavender decals over twin beds, plus a clock, side tables, and matching floor-to-ceiling closets.

"Do you care which bed I take?" Laurel asks.

I shake my head. Laurel rolls her suitcase over to one, and I take the other, beneath the wall clock. A Post-it on my bedside table shows the hotel's Wi-Fi code. I enter it into my phone.

Laurel hands me my room key. I unzip my suitcase to start organizing my clothes into one of the closets while she heads toward a narrow door just past the pillow on my bed.

"This must be the bathroom." Laurel twists the knob and peeks in. "Yep."

I make my way toward Laurel, who steps aside so I can see. There's a sink beneath a mirror, the toilet, and a small shower that looks like a test tube from last year's science class. Directly across from our door, another opens, revealing Madison.

She shrieks, and I slap my hands over both ears before I can stop myself.

"What? What is it?" Sophie-Anne's voice drifts in from their room.

"Just us," Laurel says. As she swings their door open wider, I lower my hands. "I guess we'll be sharing a bathroom."

"You scared the heck out of Madison." Sophie-Anne giggles.

"Sorry!" Laurel waves me over. "Your room looks just like ours, except you have pink flowers on your walls and we've got purple."

Madison steps past us, into the bathroom. "There's almost no counter space." She sounds as distressed as I felt when Señor L announced the changes to this trip.

While the three of them arrange their makeup, hair products, and brushes on the bathroom counter, I return to our room and grab my backpack. I haven't felt like taking out my dot diary since the airport, but now I do. Relief floods through me as I flip the pages. Everything we've done so far has followed last year's schedule. I update my task boxes with little checkmarks.

A series of sharp knocks make me look up.

"Dinnertime, girls," Mrs. West calls.

I close my diary and follow Laurel into the hall. She immediately heads toward Sophie-Anne and Madison.

Isa steps closer to me before I can join Laurel. "Thanks for earlier. No one told me if I was supposed to be on this floor or with the boys upstairs, but I'm good now."

"You're welcome," I say, even though it doesn't really feel like I did anything big. "Where did they put you?"

"2E." Isa points to a door on the opposite side of the hallway. "So I guess this is the girls-plus-Isa floor."

The rest of our group arrives before I can ask what Isa means. Together, we head down one flight of stairs to the first-floor-that's-really-the-second. At the end of the hallway, Mrs. West stops in front of two large doors.

"That over there's the community room." She points to the left door as she glances at the hotel's glossy brochure on her clipboard. "And this is the dining area."

She opens the other door, and we all file in. Two long tables divide the room. Against the far wall, platters of food are set up in neat rows on a smaller table. I quickly spot Abba. Andy, Noah-James, and other kids sit around him at the first table, chatting.

"Oh my actual gosh." Sophie-Anne nudges Laurel. She points at two teenagers sitting at the far end of the second table. A boy and a girl. Not part of our group.

"He's cute," Laurel says, but I'm still stuck on what Sophie-Anne just said. It's exactly the same phrase Laurel used on the airplane. Is Sophie-Anne who she got it from?

Madison takes the lead and we follow her to the second table, each taking a seat in front of an empty place setting, directly across from the teenagers.

The girl smiles at us.

"I know we're all hungry, so I'll keep this short," Señor L calls. "This is where we'll be having our meals, buffet-style, except on days when we're out and about."

All of this information is in my dot diary.

"This dining room is for all hotel guests, not just us. I expect y'all to be on your best behavior," Señor L continues. "Tomorrow is the official start of our program. You'll receive your team assignments in the morning, along with a school-issued tablet and a packet that has all the information you'll need to participate in the scavenger hunt, plus our afternoon lectures and field trips."

Assigned teams? My chest tightens.

"That's enough for now, though." Señor L stands. "Food's ready. Comamos."

The girl turns to us as we stand. "You are Americans?" Her words flow one into the other, like a spoken song.

"Yeah," Madison says. "From Georgia."

"The state, not the country," Sophie-Anne adds. "We're here with our Spanish class."

"Ah, vale," the girl says in Spanish. "I'm Meritxell. My brother is Xavi." Beside her, the boy gives us a small nod. He wears a striped shirt with a patch that says *FCB* on one side of his chest. It reminds me of the Lynnwood crest, minus our feathered mascot. "We are from Lleida, out west. We stay here every summer to visit family."

We introduce ourselves, then grab plates, moving to the back of the buffet table line.

I study Meritxell's shirt and the loose pants that cover lightly tanned skin, then her brown hair. Long and sleek, the ends gently curled. Xavi's hair is the same shade of brown, just shorter.

"I adore your name," Laurel tells Meritxell.

Sophie-Anne bobs her head in agreement. "How do you spell it?"

"How do you spell *your* name?" Meritxell asks.

Sophie-Anne flushes. The rest of us go quiet as Sophie-Anne answers Meritxell's question. Her voice wobbles a little as she speaks. She's probably not used to having to spell her name for anyone.

"You have a beautiful name," Meritxell says, with a smile that breaks the tension and sparks warmth in my chest.

Then Meritxell spells out her own name. She says each letter slowly, but there are no wobbles in her voice.

"It's Catalan," she explains.

Mare-eets-ell, I repeat to myself.

I don't believe in destiny—not really—but I've always liked patterns and I see one here immediately. We're in Señor *L*'s Spanish class in Barce*l*ona, staying at the same hote*l* as a girl named Meritx*ell*.

I look over at Laurel, waiting for her to connect the dots, but she doesn't turn to me. She seems to be studying Xavi. So are Madison and Sophie-Anne.

We take a few steps as the line moves up.

"Are you here on your own?" Madison asks, eyes still on Xavi.

"With our parents," Meritxell says. "Right now, they are resting."

"¿Habláis todas español?"

It's the first thing Xavi's said to us. We all look at him.

"Un poco." Madison twists a strand of hair around her finger. "We're still learning."

When it's our turn at the buffet, Meritxell and Xavi turn to fill their plates. "Xavi's English is not so great," Meritxell says as she chooses her food. "He doesn't study as much as me."

This feels like the kind of thing Dr. Talia would tell me to keep to myself, even if it's the truth. Xavi just laughs. He says something back, but I don't catch a single word. It doesn't even sound like Spanish.

"We can speak Spanish with you, if you'd like to practice," Meritxell offers.

"That'd be great." Laurel smiles at her, then surveys the platters of food.

"Try the jamón serrano." Meritxell points to the thin slices of meat on one tray. "It's a specialty."

Plates full, she and Xavi head back to our table.

"Okay, Xavi is *so* cute," Sophie-Anne loud-whispers. "How old do you think he is?"

"Fifteen," Laurel guesses. "Maybe sixteen?"

Madison reaches for a big silver fork on the tray Meritxell recommended. "We should *definitely* practice our Spanish with him sometime."

Laurel and Sophie-Anne both giggle, but my thoughts circle back to Meritxell. She was so honest and friendly. If I had a choice about who to practice Spanish with, it wouldn't be Xavi.

"Meritxell's cute, too," I chime in. "Maybe we can practice with both of them."

They all go quiet.

"*O-*kay?" Madison finally says, but she doesn't look at me as she chooses some food off the tray, then continues down the table. Sophie-Anne keeps her head down as she spears thin slices of meat, then passes the serving fork to Laurel.

Did I say something wrong?

My insides twist more when it's my turn. I don't know what *serrano* means, but *jamón* is a word I know from class. Definitely *not* kosher.

I shake my head when Laurel tries to hand me the fork.

"Oh, duh." She drops the fork back on the tray. The clang echoes in my ears.

As I fill my plate with bread, cheese, anything except meat, my gaze drifts to Abba. I wonder if he knows what *jamón* means.

Back at our table, we eat in silence. Eventually,

Sophie-Anne sets her fork down. "So, how do y'all think Señor L will pick scavenger hunt teams?"

"It'll be the four of us."

We all look at Madison.

"You think?" Laurel asks.

"Positive. It makes sense to put people together who already share a room." Madison looks at Laurel and me. "Or a bathroom."

"It'd definitely be easier to meet up and work together," says Sophie-Anne.

"Yeah," Laurel agrees.

It makes sense. I take another bite, gaze moving around the room, from Abba and Andy at one end of the second table to Emmaline at the other—anywhere but across at Meritxell.

I stop on Isa, who sits near Señor L and the other adult chaperones. There's been an odd number of students since Isa joined us, so maybe Madison's wrong.

But this seems like a problem that is out of scope.

Tomorrow, we'll get our official team assignments, I tell myself, and then I can update my schedule. Laurel and I will get to explore Barcelona together, just like we planned. Maybe it will actually be fun to be in small groups, visiting the sites I listed in my dot diary. I take another bite of dinner, finally letting myself feel excited.

Chapter Six

Day 2

I open my eyes to darkness and the steady hum of a wall-unit air conditioner, just like back home. That's where the similarities end. The wall clock *tick-tick-tick*s, my bed-sheets are scratchy, the pillow too flat under my head.

I reach for my phone on the bedside table. The screen blinks 3:53 a.m. Across from me, Laurel's mattress squeaks as she shifts in her sleep.

Curling my knees to my chest, I try to get used to the sounds of my new room. It was easier last night when Laurel and I climbed into bed after dinner, exhausted. Now I'm wide awake.

The tile floors are cool against my feet as I slip out of bed and feel around for my shoes. I grab my room key, then head out. Wall lamps bathe the hall in soft light all the way to the stairs.

I retrace my steps from last night, half expecting the community room to be locked. But the door swings open on silent hinges.

Pulling out my phone, I settle onto a couch in front of a big window. In the calm silence of this empty room, I feel like I can finally process more of yesterday.

I find the video I took on the bus. Excitement rushes through me as I take in the palm trees that line each street like a scene out of a movie. Yesterday, we sped past Spanish signs too fast for me to read. Now I can pause the video and sound out words, then study road signs with distances measured in kilometers.

Buildings rise taller as the bus nears the center of Barcelona. More people crowd the sidewalks. Pigeons scatter whenever people get too close, gray blurs against a clear blue sky.

I imagine Laurel and me exploring the Barcelona streets. We'd make up stories for each person and every building.

The video ends and I watch it again. Suddenly, the scavenger hunt doesn't seem so scary. Maybe there's even a way to weave it into a story.

I glance out the window, down at some sort of court-yard. It's surrounded by our hotel and nearby apart-ment buildings, illuminated in a dim halo of lamplight. The apartments are mostly dark, just a few windows lit up. It reminds me of Brooklyn before Mom accepted her cantor job. In New York, everyone lives on top of one another.

It's weird to feel homesick for a place that's only a handful of memories. Maybe I just miss Mom and the way her songs fill our house at just the right volume.

I check my phone. If it's 4:12 a.m. here, it'd be 10:12 p.m. back home. I double-check that I'm connected to the hotel's Wi-Fi, then send Mom a message.

Ellen Katz

Hola from Spain. Are you still awake?

Mom responds almost immediately.

Ima

Well, howdy!

Howdy? I make a face at my screen, even though Mom can't see me.

Another message pings in.

Ima

Why are you up right now?

I wish I knew the answer.

Can we video chat?

Soon, Mom's freckled face fills my screen. Her hair is red-brown like mine, but not as curly. I get my curls from Abba.

"Hi, sweetie."

"Hi," I say back. "What's with the 'howdy'?"

"I figured while you and your father were gone, I'd add some Southern phrases to my repertoire. Did you know 'Well, that just dills my pickle' is a way to say you're mad? Or it might mean you're happy." Mom shakes her head. "Maybe I should've found a different hobby."

"Probably."

I can't help smiling. While Abba and I can focus on the same thing for hours—like his drawing or my dot diary—Mom runs through hobbies fast, like songs on a playlist.

"How was your flight?"

"Looooong." I let out a puff of air.

"I bet. I remember the flight to Israel to complete my cantorial training. It was no picnic."

"But then you met Abba, so it was worth it?"

The phone bounces as Mom nods. "Yep, ja, you betcha."

"Those are *definitely* not Southern words."

"Good catch." Even Mom's laughter sounds like music. "Is Laurel with you?"

Mom cranes her neck, like she's trying to look over my shoulder.

"She's sleeping. I'm in the community room." I turn my phone around and give Mom a panoramic view.

"I see. Well, be sure to say hi for me when she wakes up."

"Okay."

Mom yawns, which makes me yawn, too. I take a mental note to add *yawns* to my list of things that are contagious, right under *grins*.

"It looks like we both could use some sleep," she says. "You should still have a couple hours before you need to get up. I'll speak with your abba about scheduling a check-in call tomorrow." Mom catches herself. "That'd be later today for you, wouldn't it? Technically, you're talking to me from the future."

"Time zones are weird."

"They are." Mom smiles. "In the meantime, try to get a little more sleep, sweetie, all right? I love you."

"Love you, too. Night, Mom."

I sit still for a few minutes after our call, savoring the quiet. When the first oranges of sunrise peek over the apartment buildings outside the window, I get up and slip back into the hall.

I nearly run into Señor L. He startles and I make a sound somewhere between a squeak and a yelp.

"Ellen! I didn't realize anyone was in there. I take it you couldn't sleep, either?"

I shake my head, trying to steady my breaths.

"Jet lag is quite normal the first few days. I'm sure some of your classmates are awake now, too—although hopefully still in their rooms." Señor L shoots me a smile. "We'll definitely go over some ground rules this morning at breakfast, like no leaving the hotel without an adult chaperone or using cell phones to navigate the city since not everyone has an international data plan. Standard stuff, so everyone's on the same page."

I stare at his T-shirt. There are no llamas this time, just a bunch of text that says, *The moment when tú start a pensar en dos languages at the mismo tiempo.*

I know what all the words mean, just not why they switch back and forth between English and Spanish. Probably another joke I don't get.

"Anyhow." A sheet of paper crinkles in his hand. "I was just fixing to post the team assignments. Feel free to take a peek, but head back to your room after, will you? No detours."

"Okay."

My stomach flutters as he moves toward the dining room door and tapes up the paper.

"Time to see if I can dormir un poco more." Señor L chuckles. "Hasta luego."

I move closer to the door and rise onto my tiptoes.

Abba's name catches my eye first, underlined at the top left corner. Señor L, Mrs. West, and Mrs. Delfina have their own top lines, with a list of student names beneath them. There are three teams with four kids each. Mrs. Delfina's has five.

I skim Abba's list and spot my name fast, then rock back on my heels.

Nothing changes when I shake my head, not even when I read it again. No matter how many times I blink or tell myself I must be dreaming, the list stays the same.

There are three other names under Abba's, forming the team I'll be on for the next two weeks. None of them are Laurel McKinley.

Chapter Seven

My alarm goes off at 8:00, sharp. As Laurel turns over in her bed, I yawn and stretch, pretending I'm waking up the same as she is.

"Mooooorning!" Laurel throws off her covers and hops out of bed. "I slept like the dead."

The dead literally can't sleep, but Laurel and her mom have said this so many times after sleepovers that I know it's a figure of speech. "Good morning."

She jogs in place. By the time I push myself up to a seated position, she's resting one leg on the metal bed frame. She reaches for her pointed toes with both hands. "Coach Vicky said I've got to stay flexible so I'm not behind when I return to the gym."

She switches legs, right as the shower turns on in the bathroom. The sound of water rushing through pipes duels with the ticking wall clock and the hum of the air conditioner.

Laurel steps away from her bed, then pulls one arm across her chest as far as it'll stretch. "Do you need to shower?"

"I'll take one tonight."

"Me too, I think." She bounces in place. Eyes sparkling, she claps her hands together and squeals. "It's our first full day in Spain, Elle!"

Something jumps in my stomach, lodging in my throat. Of course Laurel's excited. She doesn't know about the team assignments yet.

I follow her across the room to our closets. She pulls out a dress with thin shoulder straps.

"Do you like this?"

I imagine what it'd feel like to wear it, how the straps might slip down my arms and my legs would stick together. "No."

Brows scrunching, she puts it back.

"What are you going to wear today?" she asks.

"Not sure." I peer into my closet. Most of my shirts are a single color. Technically, they're made for boys, but I like them because they don't have scratchy tags on their collars. "Maybe my blue shirt. With . . . my black shorts?"

Laurel pokes her head around the closet door. "You didn't bring any skirts or dresses?"

I shake my head. I only own a few, and they hang in the deepest part of my closet, behind last year's Purim costume.

"But don't you want to dress up nice and all?"

I repeat her words in my head, but I still don't understand. "Why? We see these people every day in school."

"Not other kids. *Xavi*." She turns back to the wardrobe and lifts a skirt and blouse combo, right as the shower shuts off. "Or Meritxell for you, I guess? I didn't realize you liked girls like that."

"Oh." My face gets hot. I'd always thought it was no big deal, like all of Laurel's boy crushes, but maybe I'm wrong.

"It's cool, though." She peeks around the closet door again. "You can always borrow something of mine—or maybe we can go shopping! Madison's been to Barcelona before. She told me and Sophie there's great shopping on La Rambla."

My stomach knots up. I don't even know if shopping will be possible if we're on different teams. And when did Laurel start calling Sophie-Anne just Sophie? That's a Madison thing.

"That's the name of this huge street," Laurel continues. "Madison says it has tons of performers, plus you can walk down it all the way from the center of the city to the beach."

Laurel flits behind her closet door, and I take a breath, silently rehearsing how to tell her about the team assignments. Her pajama pants make an arc through the air, landing on her bed.

"Hey, Laur—"

The shower starts up again, cutting me off.

"*So.*" She raises her voice, and I swallow the rest of my sentence down. "What did you and Andy talk about? Yesterday, I mean. On the plane, after he and I . . ."

I pull my blue T-shirt over my head. "Changed seats?"

If Laurel feels bad about abandoning me, she doesn't say anything. "Right."

My thoughts circle back to Abba's headphones that are now mine. *Sheli and Bloom. Our story about the CEO. Kosher meals and a playlist of sleepover songs.*

The panicky feeling of waking up next to Andy. Matching silver headphones.

"Elle?"

"Graphic novels." I pull on my T-shirt and swipe at a pair of shorts. "He told Abba that he loves *Fisher's Final.*"

"Huh. I never would've guessed Andy reads stuff like that."

"Why not?"

"Well, he's a super popular basketball player."

I don't see what that has to do with liking graphic novels.

"Did he say anything else? Like about Madison, maybe?"

"He said Madison was mad because he broke up with her." The shower shuts off again, and I head back to my bed.

Laurel trails after me. "Well, sure. But did he say why?"

"No." Maybe he would have, but . . . "I didn't ask."

Laurel frowns as I sit on my bed. "Oh. That's too bad."

My fingers curl over the edge of my mattress. I'm not sure why she suddenly seems so interested in Andy.

"Y'all awake?" Sophie-Anne's voice startles us both.

"Yep. Just a sec." Laurel darts forward and opens the bathroom door. "Morrrr-ning!"

"Morning." Sophie-Anne peers into our room, her hair twisted up in a fluffy white towel. "Madison and I were about to do our makeup—"

"Just in case Xavi's in the dining room again," Madison hollers.

"Right." Laurel grins. "Just in case. Coming, Elle?"

I rock forward on my bed, then back, thinking of Xavi's sharp jaw, and the stubble under his chin. I shake my head.

"Okay, well, I'll be done in a bit. Then we can go to breakfast."

All three of their voices float back to me as they throw around words like *Sephora*, *MAC*, and *e.l.f.* Makeup sounds like a foreign language to me.

While I wait, I dig through my suitcase for my

hairbrush. Next, my backpack for my dot diary. Now that Laurel's not asking me about special clothes and Andy, I can't help thinking about the team assignments.

I stare at my diary. Under its plain black cover, there are pages filled with schedules, my personal thoughts, and pictures. In the very back, I've left space for my categories. There are lists for foods (*kosher dairy*; *kosher meat*; *pareve*; *trayf*), colors (*primary*; *secondary*; *tertiary*), things that are contagious (*grins*; *yawns*), and so on.

Dr. Talia says my categories are a coping strategy, a way for me to feel in control. To me, they just make sense. Everything has a place in my dot diary. Nothing's left out.

As I raise my brush to my head, laughter erupts from the bathroom.

"...maybe even invite him to figure out clues with us."

My brush hits a snarl. I wince, then use my fingers to loosen the tangle.

"Ready, Elle?" Laurel reappears. Her lips are bright and glossy, cheeks a rosy pink.

She used to only wear this much makeup for gymnastics meets.

I slip my dot diary into my backpack, then follow her out the door.

As we head downstairs with Sophie-Anne and Madison, I remember one of the first categories I ever created, all the way back in third grade on the day I met Laurel: *Time*.

The list only has two items on it, but they're both important.

1. Before: When I didn't know anyone on my first day at Lynnwood.
2. After: Laurel got assigned to be my guide, then we became friends.

I'd always thought of "before" as the worst, because I'd just moved to Georgia and didn't know anyone. "After" is when everything fell into place and Laurel became my best-and-only.

It's the opposite now, because "before" means Laurel still thinks we'll be on the same team.

Downstairs, kids gather in the hall, all studying the notice taped to the dining room door.

"Look!" Sophie-Anne squeals.

I press my arms hard against my sides.

Laurel lets Sophie-Anne pull her forward, and there's nothing to do but follow. No matter what Dr. Talia says about coping strategies and control, *Time* is a category that makes me feel helpless.

Every step brings me closer to an "after" that's going to be awful.

Chapter Eight

Classmates gather in front of the list, and Laurel comes to a stop behind them. She rises to her tiptoes to see over their heads. Sophie-Anne copies her.

I inch forward but freeze as Sophie-Anne squeals a second time in the span of a minute. "Madison was right!"

"But why didn't they put all four of us together?" Laurel asks as she twists her necklace. "It's me, Sophie-Anne, and Madison, with Cody Mack."

Sophie-Anne makes a face, and I shove my hands deep in my pockets.

"That makes no sense." Madison looks between Laurel and me. "Why would they separate roommates? They didn't split up Emmaline and Clara or Sully and Tess."

I've been wondering this for hours.

Laurel frowns. "I'm so sorry, Elle."

"All right, everyone," Señor L calls from the dining room. "Come on in and eat up. We have an exciting day ahead of us."

We enter with the others, then grab our plates and line up for the buffet table. Every second of silence makes my shoulders tense harder.

I look around the dining room as I fill my plate. Andy sits next to Noah-James at one table, just like yesterday, while Abba's farther up, across from Mrs. West and Mrs. Delfina. Isa is at the head of the other table, sitting alone. I hesitate, looking from Isa to the boys, then to Abba.

Laurel nudges me. "Sit with us."

Shoulders relaxing, I follow her to the spot where we sat last night. The seats across from us are empty today. No Meritxell and Xavi.

"Buenos días," Señor L says as soon as we take our seats. "Or bon dia, as many of the locals say. I hope you're all excited about your new teams."

Laurel squeezes my hand under the table. I squeeze back.

"If you didn't end up with the people you were hoping for, consider it a chance to get to know some of your classmates better."

I glance toward the other table. Andy seems to be listening to Señor L, but Noah-James's eyes are on his phone.

"There'll also be plenty of opportunities to spend time with your friends at the afternoon lectures and field trips, plus during the siestas and dinners right after them," Señor L continues.

Across the room, Noah-James sets his phone down and digs into his food. Mouth full, he says something to Andy. Andy turns, and we're suddenly looking right at each other. My gaze skitters away, toward Abba and the other adult chaperones.

"I still don't get it," Madison says as Señor L goes over the ground rules he mentioned when we ran into each other earlier. He also lets us know the chaperones have subway passes for everyone and can buy us things like admission tickets. Our parents paid in advance for things like this as part of our trip tuition.

He tells us to come get an info packet and assemble into our teams once we've finished eating. Madison keeps talking without missing a beat. "If they were going to make us do small groups, at least let us choose who we want to work with."

"Right?" Sophie-Anne sighs. "This feels like school, just in a different location."

I'm about to tell her this trip technically *is* school when Abba catches my eye.

Opportunities. Small groups.

Suddenly, the words rearrange themselves into a complete sentence. They're no longer in a Southern accent but one that's airy Israeli.

My body goes hot. As Abba turns back to the moms, I remember our talk at the airport.

He said there'd be opportunities to be more on my own. Times when my classmates and I might be in small groups.

I stare at my plate.

What if Abba knew I was supposed to be on Laurel's team but then he asked Señor L to switch me after I said I didn't need space?

My fault.

I force myself to eat something, taking small bites. Kids chatter around me. Noise builds like a crescendo in one of Mom's songs.

This is all my fault.

I try to think of something else, like Dr. Talia's tips to combat overwhelm. But my breath catches. My chest feels tight.

"Ellen? Hi." I look up. Isa stands across the table from me. I stare at purple hair, then a silver stud in the cartilage of one ear.

I swallow hard. "Hey . . ."

"You know who our other teammates are, right?"

"Laurel, let's move down a bit," Sophie-Anne calls.

I blink fast, trying to untangle the two sentences.

Laurel waves at me, then scoots toward her team as Cody Mack drops into a seat across from them. He runs a hand through his shaggy blond hair while I repeat Isa's question to myself. Once each word connects to the next and the sentence finally makes sense, I nod.

"Cool. You want to go meet up with them?"

"No." I don't even care if being honest makes me sound rude right now.

To my surprise, Isa laughs. "Me neither, if they're the two I think they are. But we should probably go anyway."

Isa's right. Unfortunately.

Slowly, I grab my backpack, throwing one last glance at Laurel. She and Sophie-Anne sit shoulder to shoulder, eyes on the packet Señor L just handed out.

I lead Isa to Andy and Noah-James at the other table. A few seats away, Emmaline waves her hands as she talks to her teammates, just like Mom does when she's excited. Light glints off a silver ring on her pinkie finger. My eyes follow the dancing sparkle.

"Nu, metukah." Abba appears. "Ready to get started?"

Eyes still on Emmaline's ring, I don't respond.

"Señor L gave us our info packets." A rapid flutter of paper draws my attention toward my new team. Noah-James waves the stapled sheets so fast it creates a breeze.

"And a school tablet." Andy holds it up. "Want to go to the community room? It's probably quieter."

"I'm down," Isa says.

Without a word, I follow Isa and the boys out of the dining room, Abba trailing behind us.

The boys claim the community room couch. Isa and I sit down in a pair of armchairs across from them, separated by a coffee table. I hug my backpack to my chest like a shield.

Only Abba stays standing. "I'll be in my room: 3B. Once you've decided on your first destination, come get me."

The door clicks closed.

"So..." Andy places the school tablet and info packets on the coffee table. "We should probably introduce ourselves."

Noah-James slouches into the couch cushion. His messy brown hair falls over one eye, but he doesn't lift a hand to brush it away. "Dude, we already know each other."

"Not all of us do." Andy glances at Isa.

I remember when Laurel and I first met, in Lynnwood's front office. Her hair was longer then, woven into two perfect French braids. She seemed to know everyone as she guided me to my first class, introducing me to each kid we passed in the hallway. Soon, I knew everyone, too, all thanks to Laurel.

It's only been a few minutes, but I miss her already.

"I'll go first," Andy says. "I'm Andy Zhang. I'm thirteen, and, uh..." He presses his lips together for a moment. "I have a little sister and play basketball. I guess that's about it."

"What are your pronouns?" Isa asks.

"Sorry, what?"

"You know, like *he* and *she*," Isa says. "What words do you use?"

"*Oh.*" Andy's brows rise. "*He*, I guess."

"Cool." Isa crosses one leg over the other. "I'm Isa Martinez. I'm thirteen, and my family just moved from the Bronx in New York. I have two younger sisters and a baby brother, so I can recite basically every Disney movie by heart. I'm also really good at fixing the things they break."

So that explains the *Emperor's New Groove* reference.

"My pronouns are *they*, *them*, and *their*," Isa continues.

"*They* is for a group of people," Noah-James cuts in, "not just one."

"Nope, not always," Isa shoots back.

I flinch, then look down fast, hoping no one will notice. Maybe it's because we're sitting close to each other, but Isa's voice rings in my ears. Too sharp. Too loud.

"People use it all the time when they don't know the gender of the person they're talking about," Isa explains. "That's how I use it, too."

There's a category for pronouns in my dot diary, a page I created when I started taking Spanish. It's got entries for English and Spanish, plus Hebrew. But each entry only has two sets of words: one for boys, the other for girls.

They, *them*, and *their* don't fit on my lists. Not in any language.

"Because you're not a boy or a girl?" Andy asks. "That's what you said at the airport, right?"

"Yeah."

I squeeze my backpack tighter.

Noah-James drops his legs onto the coffee table, narrowly missing the tablet. "So why are you staying on the girls' floor then?"

"Because people don't know what to do with someone different from what they're used to." Isa shrugs. "They figure it out eventually, or they don't. Not my problem."

Still too loud. I bite down on the inside of my cheek.

"All right, well..." It's a relief when Noah-James clears his throat. "Anyhow. I'm Noah-James Gibson III, but my teammates call me Gibs. Y'all can, too. I'm thirteen, same as everyone, and number twenty-one on the court. Last season wasn't the greatest. I had a hard time concentrating, but then I found out I have ADHD so that probably explains it." He looks over at Andy. "But we're gonna kill it this year, right?"

I wonder if he has an individualized education plan set up to help him at school like I do, but the question sticks in my throat.

"Totally," Andy says.

"Pronouns?" Isa asks.

For a moment, I think Noah-James—Gibs—might refuse, but he just rolls his eyes. "I'm a guy. Obviously."

"So *he, him, his.* Good to know." Isa turns to me. "What about you?"

"Ellen," I say. "Ellen Katz. I'm thirteen, and..." Suddenly, I can't remember what the others shared. I grip my backpack tighter. If Laurel were here, she could step in.

"My best friend, Laurel, and I have sleepovers on Saturday nights," I say in a rush to fill the growing silence. Then I remember that Isa's new and doesn't know everyone yet. "She's the girl I was sitting next to at breakfast, plus dinner last night."

"The one she's attached to like white on—" Gibs goes quiet when Andy elbows him.

Isa acts like nothing happened, doesn't even look at them. "Any brothers or sisters?"

"No. But I watch Disney movies with my dad. He's an artist." Out of the corner of my eye, I see Andy nod. "And I use *she*, *her*, and *hers* for pronouns—but I also like yours."

Isa grins. "No reason you can't use both."

Before I can ask Isa how that'd work, Andy leans forward and reaches for the info packets.

"We should probably get started. Everyone ready?"

I place my backpack on the floor as Andy hands out the packets. My mouth feels dry. My dot diary can't help me anymore now that this new version of our trip has officially started.

PRIMERA PISTA

Soy el arquitecto de la luz y el silencio,

el hombre que creó

los famosos panots de las calles.

~

Busquen las pinturas murales,

un museo en un ático,

y las chimeneas guerreras

en el Paseo de Gracia.

~

¡Buena suerte!

Chapter Nine

"The clue's in *Spanish*." Gibs stares at the first page.

"On a trip to Spain? Shocker." But Andy doesn't seem shocked as he flips to the instructions section. "It looks like there are three clues total, but we have to solve the first before Señor L will give us the second one. Then we have to solve that to get the third. The only real due date is this Friday, when we need to finish the first two clues. Then we have to solve the third one before we leave next week. Plus stuff like no asking our chaperone for help or sharing clue info with the other teams."

"Sounds complicated," Gibs says.

"Honestly?" Isa sighs. "It just sounds like a scavenger hunt to me."

Andy studies his packet. "It also says we need to take

pictures at the clue locations to prove we actually visited them."

He reaches for the school tablet. "Want to get started?"

"Sure. But hey." Gibs sits up. "Your last name is Martinez."

Isa looks back at him. "Yeah, so?"

"So . . . can't you just translate it for us?"

"What's your last name again? Gibson?" Isa's head tilts to one side. "What part of the world is your family from? Like, before they moved to Georgia."

"Um?" Gibs blinks. "Scotland, I think. And Ireland."

"Do you know Scottish or Irish?"

My gaze shifts from Isa to Gibs just in time to see the tips of his ears flush pink. "No?"

"Katz is German," I blurt out, "and I definitely don't know that language."

Everyone's looking at me now. Pulse racing, I clamp my mouth shut. Out of the corner of my eye, I catch a thumbs-up from Isa.

"Okay, fine." Gibs flops back onto the couch. "Google Translate also works."

Everyone else goes quiet. I flip through the packet fast, studying our new schedule. Each morning is free for us to search for scavenger hunt clues, then Señor L has scheduled either a lecture or field trip every afternoon. There's a lecture on the history of Barcelona, another on Spanish culture, and so on. Plus trips to places like Plaça Nova and the Picasso Museum. I'm tempted to reach into my backpack and update my diary, but I make myself turn back to the clue on page one.

It'd probably be easier to translate the clue all at once, but I can't help reading through it to see which words I recognize first.

I already know *luz* means "light" and *silencio* is "silence." *Calle* is "street," and there are a couple of words I can guess because they look similar to English. A few words sound familiar, like maybe we learned them in class. I write down as many English translations as I can.

This reminds me of Saturday sleepovers, when Laurel and I would listen to Spanish music, then Google Translate the lyrics so we'd know what each song was about. I wonder if her team figured the clue out fast and already left the hotel.

I push the thought away and decide to translate each remaining word one at a time. That's the rhythm I prefer, even if it's slower. My hands tingle as each new translation gets me closer to the answer.

"Okay, I give up," Gibs groans before I'm even halfway done. "This one part came out as 'warrior chimneys,' which makes the kind of sense that doesn't."

"I got 'warrior chimneys,' too, actually," Andy says. "This clue is confusing."

I study my sheet but keep quiet. I haven't made it to that part yet.

"Here's what I got," Andy says. " 'I am the architect of light and silence, the man who created the street' ... um, so ... I couldn't find a translation for *panots*."

"Same here," says Isa. "I looked it up, and the first result said *panot* means 'bald' in Tagalog."

Gibs snorts.

I return to Google Translate, but it gives me the same result. I switch to regular Google, adding *Barcelona* to my search criteria.

The answer stares back at me. It even comes with rows of photos.

My teammates are quiet, eyes on their phones and the tablet. If Laurel were here, I could hand over my phone and she'd tell everyone what I found. I'm not sure what to do on my own.

I rock in my chair, just a little so no one can tell what I'm doing. But the longer I keep myself still, the more my distress builds up. I need my rocking to calm me down.

"Did you find something?" Isa's voice is quieter now.

I nod, but don't say anything.

"Can I see?"

Isa extends a hand, and I pass over my phone.

As Isa studies my screen, I take a moment to try out *they*, *them*, *their* pronouns in my head.

They read a definition off my phone, then click on a photo. It enlarges, and *their* eyes widen.

It's actually not hard to use different pronouns.

"Ellen figured it out." Isa's voice rises. They show the boys the photo before handing me back my phone. "It looks like it's a type of tile."

"So this guy made fancy sidewalk designs," Gibs says.

"I guess?" Andy glances back down at his clue sheet. "If that translation's right, it says, 'I am the architect of light and silence, the man who created the famous street tiles. Look for wall paintings, a museum in an attic, and warrior chimneys on the grace walk. Good luck.'"

He looks up. "It's like a riddle."

"Are we sure the end of this is right, though?" Gibs asks. "Like what the heck even *is* a 'warrior chimney'?"

"No clue. An architect, street tiles, and grace. Plus wall paintings and an attic museum." Andy taps his knee with a finger as he lists off each part of the clue. My finger twitches, wanting to copy him. "What do they all have to do with each other?"

My gaze jumps from Andy to Gibs to Isa as they all throw out ideas.

Andy thinks the architect also made the paintings and chimneys.

Searching Barcelona museums could lead us to the architect, according to Gibs.

Isa says the warrior chimneys might be a metaphor of some sort.

Maybe I should help them guess, but I can't figure out how to join in their conversation now that they're talking loudly and all at once. Without Laurel, everything feels off.

"Found something!" Andy says, eyes back on the tablet. "There's this guy who designed a bunch of buildings in Barcelona, plus street tiles. His name's Antoni Gaudí."

That name sounds familiar.

"Cool," Isa says. "But what about the other parts, like the 'grace walk'?"

There's too much talking for me to concentrate. I lift my hands, then force them back down before they reach my ears.

"Sounds like a church."

Andy and Isa stop talking. We all look over at Gibs.

" 'Light and silence'? It sounds like a chapel, right?" Gibs says. "Plus, churches have tons of tiles, and my pastor is always preaching 'eternal grace-this' and 'grace everlasting-that.' It fits."

I almost drop my phone in the rush to open my backpack.

The other kids go quiet, watching me.

I pull out my dot diary and flip through the pages. This time, my words come out in a rush of excitement. "We're supposed to visit a church—or we were." I point to the page dated for next Wednesday.

Andy squints at my diary. "La Sagrada Família?"

"Yes." I nod. "The architect is Antoni Gaudí."

Andy types something into the tablet. "That could be it. Some of these articles call it the most famous place in Barcelona."

Gibs hops up, then takes a bow. "You're welcome."

"Technically," Isa says, "Ellen's the one who figured it out."

I fix my eyes on my diary entry, secretly pleased.

"Whatever." Gibs flops back down beside Andy. "I still helped."

"What do y'all think?" Andy asks Isa and me. "Should we visit the church?"

"Sure," Isa says. "It sounds right to me."

Gibs pumps his fist in the air.

"Ellen?" Andy asks.

I glance down at my sheet, studying each line of the clue again, my confidence growing by the second. The scavenger hunt is just last year's trip in a slightly different format. It has to be.

"I also think we should go to the church."

Gibs hoots and runs a circle around the room, one

hand bouncing like he's dribbling a basketball. Arms up, he makes a *swoosh* sound as he scores an imaginary basket.

Andy ignores him. Eyes on the tablet, he takes notes on his clue sheet. "It looks like it's a quick subway ride from here. There's a fee to go inside. We can ask Mr. Katz to order tickets before we leave."

We exit the community room together. I pause in front of the dining area, but it's quiet now. No sounds of Laurel, or anyone.

Halfway down the hall, Isa turns back to me. "Coming, Ellen?"

"Yes." I sprint toward them, and we head upstairs together to get Abba.

Chapter Ten

Tickets bought, my team leaves the hotel with Abba. The humid air fills my throat. I almost expect to see a coil of steam when I exhale.

"The nearest metro station is about a block away," Andy tells us as we wait to cross the street. "A guy at the hotel mentioned it after dinner last night."

"Xavi, right?" Isa asks. "I saw you two talking. He and his sister were chatting with some of the other kids at dinner. They seem nice."

During a sleepover, Laurel told me the best way to feel comfortable around other kids is to join in their conversation. I try to imagine what Laurel would say here.

"My friend thought Xavi was cute."

Gibs laughs even though I didn't say anything remotely funny. "She can get in line."

As soon as the walk sign flickers on, Andy takes off.

"Hey, Mr. Andy," Abba calls. "Where's the fire?"

"Sorry!" Andy waits for us to catch up, then guides us down a wide pedestrian lane with cars rolling past on either side.

I look back toward Hotel El Búho. As the owl stares down at me, I remember the story Laurel and I came up with yesterday: the Big Chicken of Barcelona. I pull out my phone, zoom in, and take a quick photo.

A few runners jog past, their shoes slapping a rhythm against the pavement. The scent of fresh bread drifts from a nearby bakery as I glance up at the buildings beyond the car lanes on either side of us. My gaze snags on a red and yellow striped flag that hangs from a balcony. It whips back and forth in the same breeze that blows my hair into my eyes. I let my phone capture all the people, each building—recording everything—so I can watch it later.

Abba hands us each a two-week, unlimited-ride metro pass when we get to the subway station.

As we head down a set of stairs, Abba steps beside me. "Hakol beseder?"

I shrug. The light, the heat, all the people: There are so many things to see, hear, and even smell. I already feel tired.

"Did you bring your headphones?"

I grip the stairs' railing harder. "Yes."

"Use them if you need to, metukah."

Abba is just trying to look out for me, but if I slide on my headphones, my team might ask why I'm wearing them. It's not a secret, but my throat gets tight just thinking about explaining sensory overwhelm in the middle of a busy subway station.

As we gather with the others at the bottom of the stairs, I change the subject. "Do you remember how to use the train, from when we lived in New York?"

"I do." But Abba doesn't say anything else.

"He's not supposed to help us, remember?" Gibs turns to Abba. "You just follow us around and make sure we don't get hit by a bus or something, right?"

"Something like that." Abba chuckles.

"We'll be fine," Isa says. "My family took the subway all the time in New York."

They lead the way, toward a row of silver gates. At some point between the hotel and subway station, they put in an earbud, but just one. The cord dangles, a string of white against their black T-shirt. Isa feeds their pass into a slot in front of the gate, which whirs and spits the ticket back out. Then the gate opens.

The rest of us copy Isa, then follow them into the station. When the tunnel forks, Isa pauses for Andy to read off directions he jotted down on his clue sheet.

I trail behind at the back of our group, memorizing everything he says:

Blue line: L5.

Direction: Vall d'Hebron.

One stop between us and La Sagrada Família.

We get on the next train that pulls up. I find the emptiest corner, then press my back against the car's smooth wall. Nearby, my teammates and Abba hold on to a silver pole for balance as the train shoots forward.

A minute later, a woman's tinny voice crackles over a speaker. "Próxima parada: Sagrada Família."

"Dang." Gibs whistles.

"Yeah." Andy shields his eyes with one hand. "The travel sites all said it was big, but..."

"...this thing's *massive*," Isa finishes for him.

I glance up. The church is both tall and wide, with four spires rising to dizzying heights. Construction cranes hover overhead, although I can't immediately see what part of the building needs work. The bright blue sky stands out against the church's off-white exterior. Some parts look old, the texture of a dried-up honeycomb, others newer, with smoother stone.

Tourists line up. There are so many more people here

than in our hotel's neighborhood. Voices rise and fall. The heat makes my sleeves stick to my arms.

I look down and study the smooth sidewalk tiles. My teammates' voices join the buzz of tourists. I thrum my fingers against my leg, wishing I was back in my quieter hotel room.

A hand waves in front of my face. I blink fast, shake my head a little, then look up at Gibs.

"What?"

"Aren't you gonna even look at it?" he asks as the line moves forward.

"I did." And then I looked down to avoid overwhelm, but I keep that part to myself.

Abba shows our electronic tickets to a worker at an enormous wood door.

The moment we get inside, everyone freezes. My teammates' eyes move from the pews ahead of us to the stained glass on the church's windows. Stone columns rise hundreds of feet above me. My eyes travel up one big column, then back down another.

"Wow," Andy whispers.

Gibs nods. Isa removes their earbud.

Tourists walk up and down pew aisles. Around columns and under stained-glass windows. It's just like outside, with one big difference: The noise stays at a soft hum.

"Want to split up and see if we can find the other

parts of the clue?" Andy pulls out his sheet. "And don't forget to take pics."

I look at Abba as we split off, wondering who he'll follow. But he ambles toward the next row of pews, taking pictures with his phone.

I follow Isa to one side of the church, where light pours through the stained-glass windows. Shades of green and blue dance across the floor, the pews, even my arms.

La luz y el silencio. Light and silence.

Isa walks ahead of me, eyes on the ceiling. Thinking of Isa as they, them, and their hasn't been hard, even if I don't get how to fit them into my diary's pronouns category. But knowing what Isa meant when they said they're not a boy or a girl? That part is like our scavenger hunt clue: I understand each word on its own but not what it means as a whole.

Isa looks back at me and I pretend to study the ceiling, too. I should be looking for things like wall paintings and warrior chimneys, but the moment Isa turns away I aim my phone at my free hand. I flick my wrist. Warmth forms in my stomach and my arms tingle as the light dances across my skin. I turn my hand more slowly, savoring each blue and green shimmer.

Dr. Talia calls it stimming whenever I rock my body, flap my hands, or focus on something shiny. It's a way of centering myself. I rock to calm down and flap to let my happiness out. Stimming feels as natural as breathing, but it still gets me weird looks.

I click off my phone and catch up with Isa, passing a man and a woman along the way.

"How the heck did Gaudí build this?" Isa murmurs. "Like, do architects have to figure out what materials to use, or do they just come up with the design?"

My gaze rises, taking in all of the dramatic architecture in a spectrum of colors. I honestly have no idea. All I know is Laurel would adore this, but there's no sign of her team anywhere.

"Because this is *amazing*," Isa continues, voice rising. I glance over at the couple behind us, worried they'll shush Isa, or ask us to leave for being too loud.

But Isa's next words are quieter. "My family goes to Mass every week and our church is nice, but this is next level."

I nod. "If my temple looked like this, I'd be too distracted to pay attention during services."

"No joke." Isa grins.

As we head toward the center of the church, I spot a mosaic on the floor, in front of a raised platform. It reminds me of my temple's bimah, except instead of Torah scrolls behind a curtain, there's a crucifix.

The couple's conversation drifts over to us as we walk.

"This never gets old, does it?" The man speaks English, his accent nasal and British.

"Never," the woman agrees.

"I'm going to snap a pic of that floor tile in case it's what the clue meant." Isa heads away from me.

I keep my eyes on them as they crouch down to study the tile, but something feels off.

"I do hope we can make time to see other Gaudí sites this go-around," the woman says.

My ears perk up at the Gaudí mention. I watch the couple out of the corner of my eye, keeping a few feet ahead of them.

"Then let's," the man says. "We can grab a bite, then make our way to Passeig de Gràcia. It's a scenic walk, as I recall."

I freeze, and the couple stops fast to avoid running into me.

One deep, calming breath, then I sprint over to Isa. "We need to find Andy and Gibs."

"Why? What's wrong?"

I scan the church, pulse pounding in my throat. But the boys aren't in sight, and there's nothing calm about the words that tumble out next.

"I got the clue wrong." My voice rises without my permission. "We're not in the right place."

Chapter Eleven

We weave around tourists on our way to the other side of the church.

If I were making a list, I'd put this under *Things That Are My Fault*, along with the team assignments. My hands ball into fists, nails digging into each palm.

At first, there's no sign of the boys. Then the slap of sneakers breaks through the low murmur of tourists as Gibs sprints toward us. Andy isn't far behind.

Gibs comes to a stop in front of us. "Find anything good?"

Isa glances at me, and I look down fast. "Not really," they say. "What about you guys?"

"Much grace. Very wow." Gibs shrugs. "We also found the museum."

My hands relax a little. Maybe I wasn't wrong about the clue after all.

"I'm not sure it's right, though," Andy says, and my hope shrinks. "It was called a sacristy, not a museum. It had a few religious items, but it definitely wasn't in an attic."

"I took pics anyway." Gibs waves his phone.

Light pours out of the windows. On this side of the church, everything's red, orange, and yellow. I don't twist my hand to watch the sparkles.

I find my voice. "Not right."

"Why?" Isa asks.

If Laurel were here, she'd know what to say. I glance toward Abba, but he's still seated. He looks up and studies the stained-glass windows to his left, then back down toward his lap. Probably using one of his phone's art apps to sketch what he just saw.

I keep my eyes on him, wishing I could repeat the couple's conversation. But words get tangled in my head, especially when I'm the center of attention.

"Not right," I repeat, but I know it's not enough to make them understand. I take a breath, finally managing to get the rest of the words out. "The clue...it was talking about a different location."

"Like, the guy made another huge church somewhere?" Gibs squints up at the ceiling.

I shrug. Glance down.

"It sounds like we need to do more research," Isa says.

Gibs groans extra loud, then dodges before Andy can elbow him.

"I think Ellen might be right." Andy's clue sheet rustles in his hands. "The museum part already felt wrong. Does anyone see painted walls anywhere?"

I steal a look at my teammates, who scan the church, then shake their heads.

"What about the panots?" Andy asks.

Same response.

"Maybe," Isa says, "we're supposed to look outside for the tiles. The clue said 'panots de las *calles*,' right?"

That's the part that felt off to me when Isa was studying the floor tile.

"Yeah." Andy looks back down at the clue sheet. "It definitely says street panots."

"Not right." I want to say so much more.

"What's not right?" Gibs asks.

"Hey." Isa turns to me. "You were looking down when we were waiting in line. Did the sidewalks have designs on them?"

I shake my head.

"So maybe they're on the other side of the church," Gibs says. "It doesn't mean we're in the wrong place."

"But 'Gracia' does..." I force out.

Gibs waves his hand in a big arc. "How does this *not* say 'grace' to you?"

"Hey, chill," Andy tells Gibs. "She's just trying to help."

Andy looks over at me, and I drop my gaze fast. "Why doesn't 'gracia' work, Ellen?"

Speaking to the floor helps the words form. "I heard a couple of people talking about places Gaudí designed. They said some were on Passeig de Gràcia."

"Huh." Andy's clue sheet rustles again. "*Oh*. The *G* is capitalized. I totally missed that."

"Let me guess," Isa says. "This church isn't on Passeig de Gràcia."

"Nope," Andy says. "I'm pretty sure we would've noticed if it was."

As he and Isa continue talking, Gibs shuffles closer to me. "Hey."

When I don't say anything, he sighs. "I'm sorry, okay? I'm just annoyed that we chose the wrong place and won't have time to go anywhere else today."

I give him a quick nod. It's not hot inside the church, but my face burns. Gibs is mad because I led us to the wrong place on the very first day. The others might be, too.

"It's almost noon," Andy says. "Want to grab lunch, then do some more research back at the hotel before Señor L's lecture?"

Fixing my mess-up is the last thing I want to do. But

when Gibs and Isa both nod, I feel like I have no choice but to copy them.

Two metro stops later, we climb the subway station steps and head back to the hotel.

Guilt weighs me down, from my shoulders to my dragging feet. All I want to do is hide in my room.

We enter the hotel, and I rub my eyes, trying to adjust to the dimmer lighting.

"¡Bona tarda!"

Meritxell comes into view halfway down the hallway. She closes a hotel room door, then approaches us. "O buenas tardes, si preferís el español."

"Buenas tardes" if we prefer Spanish? Then what language is "bona tarda"?

Meritxell glances at me, and the question sticks in my throat.

"Hola," Andy and Isa say together. They glance at each other, then break out into grins.

Meritxell speaks again, but Andy shakes his head before I can turn back to her.

"Lo siento," Andy says, "I heard you say 'divertido' and 'ciudad,' but that's all I caught."

Meritxell switches to English. "I asked, did you have fun today in the city?"

I nod along with the others as they tell her about our visit to La Sagrada Família.

"A good choice," Meritxell says. "My family attends Mass there each summer." She lowers her voice a little. "Although sometimes the services are very long, and I get bored."

Isa laughs. "Same here!"

This time when I look up, Meritxell smiles. I can't tell if it's meant for Isa or me, but my chest flutters anyway.

"Yeah, but Ellen picked the wrong place," Gibs says. "So we kinda wasted the day."

A stab of guilt. The fluttering sputters to a stop.

Andy frowns. "I don't think that's the right way to—"

"Please excuse me, I need to go—" Meritxell pauses as her words overlap with Andy's.

They both go quiet, like neither knows whether they should finish their sentence.

"Actually, maybe you could help us with something. . . ." All eyes turn toward Isa. "We're trying to figure out a clue about Gaudí for our scavenger hunt."

"A clue?" Meritxell takes a small step toward the door but hesitates. "I'm sorry. I don't know what 'scavenger hunt' means."

"Una pista," Andy explains, then looks back at us. "Um. Does anyone know how to say 'scavenger hunt' in Spanish? Actually, just a sec."

He pulls out his phone. "I'll check Google Translate."

Abba steps forward before Andy can type anything. "My intrepid travelers. It looks like Meritxell might have somewhere she needs to be."

"Okay, yeah. Sorry." Andy hops aside, and bumps into me.

I startle and back up, knocking into the hallway wall.

"Sorry!" he says again.

And it's not so much that Andy touched me as a bunch of things all piling up at once.

The itchy, sticky heat.

A noisy subway and tourist-packed streets.

Getting the clue wrong.

Meritxell's smile.

"Yes, thank you." Meritxell slips past us. "Adéu. See you later."

"Are you okay, Ellen?" Andy asks.

"Just tired." A half-truth is still true. Kind of.

"Saaaame." Gibs makes a sound that may or may not be a real yawn. "Maybe we can take a nap. What if we save the research until after Señor L's lecture, Mr. Katz?"

"That's entirely up to you. I'm just here to make sure you don't get hit by a bus."

I understood that joke, but I can't bring myself to smile.

"I'm actually tired, too." Andy heads toward the stairs. "We can always do more research during the official siesta time later."

One floor up, Isa and I pause on the landing.

"Let me know if you need anything," Abba calls. Gibs takes off, too.

Andy lingers a couple of steps above us. "I was thinking I could set up a team chat. Then we can talk when we're all in the hotel and don't even need to be in the same room."

"Sounds cool." Isa's already got their phone out, so I pull mine out, too. I go through the motions as we share our numbers with Andy, promising to text later.

In my room, the rumble of the air conditioner greets me. It's noisy but familiar compared to the rest of Barcelona. For once, I'm grateful Laurel's not around so I don't have to tell her about my day yet.

I drop into bed and pull out my diary. If I update it with all the canceled events, it'd look more confusing than a Barcelona subway map. It'd also take forever to completely start over. I push it away.

I'm too tired. Heavy-feeling. Overwhelmed. Everything's wrong. I don't even want to watch the video I took. I curl onto my side and close my eyes, wishing I could start this whole trip over.

Chapter Twelve

The slam of a door jolts me awake. My room floods with light.

"Crap." Laurel spots me in bed. "I thought you'd be up by now. Sorry!"

I rub my eyes. "What time is it?"

"Like eight thirty."

"*Eight* thirty?" I stare at her.

"Yeah. At least this happened today and not tomorrow during the group dinner."

"Group dinner?"

"Señor L told us about it during today's lecture. We're all going to a restaurant together tomorrow night." She gives me a small smile. "You were out cold when I came in earlier. I was going to wake you up before the lecture, but your dad said to let you sleep when he came down to check on you. He said something about overload?"

"I guess." My head still feels foggy. It takes a moment for the day to come back to me, but now the heaviness I felt earlier makes more sense. Whenever too much sensory stuff hits me all at once, I need to reset someplace quiet.

"Your dad said you'd need something to eat. . . ."

For the first time, I notice the plate in her hands.

My stomach growls. Laurel grins as she passes me the food. As she hands me utensils and a napkin, I study the food on the plate, looking for anything trayf.

"It's all kosher. Your dad helped me pick everything out."

Relieved, I dig in as she skips over to her bed.

"Señor L's lecture was super boring," Laurel says. "Maybe you should pretend to sleep through the rest of them."

I glance up, ready to explain how my individualized education plan doesn't give me a free pass to get out of boring stuff. But my mouth is full, and Laurel continues before I can swallow.

"Meritxell said she missed seeing you at dinner tonight."

I cough, swallowing a chunk of potato whole. "She said that?"

"Yep." Laurel slides a purse off her shoulder, then drops onto her bed. "How was your day?"

"I messed up the first clue, so we visited the wrong place."

"Oh no, Elle. That sucks. But it's only the first day. You've still got plenty of time." Laurel unbuttons the top flap of her purse and pulls out her phone. She crosses her legs beneath her skirt, settling in.

My eyes stay on her purse. It's yellow, a primary color. Her favorite bags are usually secondary colors (like purple) or tertiary (pink, mint green).

"Is that new?"

"Yep! I bought it at this souvenir stand by the beach. Isn't it cute?"

I'm not really sure what qualifies as cute, so I change the subject. "Your team went to the beach to look for the first clue?"

"Well... we haven't started the scavenger hunt yet."

I stare at her. "You didn't even translate the first clue?"

"Nope, not yet." Laurel looks up from her phone. "Like I said, it's only day one. We've got lots of time. Plus, we all really wanted to check out the beach."

It's almost Tuesday, and we need to have two clues done by Friday. That doesn't sound like a lot of time to me, definitely not enough time to waste a day at the beach, or by visiting the wrong place.

Then my thoughts shift to the last thing she said. "*Everyone* wanted to see the beach?"

"Well okay, Cody wasn't thrilled. He wanted us to translate the clue, but Madison held a vote. She said the majority should decide, just like in elections."

I'm not sure that's actually how elections work, but my phone buzzes before I can say so. I accept a message request from Andy, and a stream of texts appear in our new group chat.

Andy
Test

Isa (they/them)
It's aliiiiive

Andy
Does it work for you, Ellen and Gibs?

There are too many messages to read now, including some from Gibs. I set my plate on the bedside table, then tap out a quick reply.

Ellen
Hi. I missed these while I was asleep. It works for me.

"Oh my actual gosh, Elle!" Laurel bounces on her bed. "I just had the *best* idea."

I set my plate aside, trying to remember what we

were just talking about. A new purse, the beach, and Cody Mack. "What's your idea?"

"It's soooo good. I can't believe I didn't think of it sooner." Laurel joins me on my bed. "Want to guess?"

"Just tell me."

"Okay." Laurel practically vibrates with excitement. "You should ask to switch teams."

My phone buzzes again, and my thoughts take off in different directions.

"I . . . um, that would be—"

"Perfect, right?" Laurel's brows rise.

Another notification. I force myself to look up from my phone, back to Laurel.

"It would be great," I say, which is true. I want to spend time with her more than anything. "But I don't think Señor L will just let kids change teams."

"Maybe not, but he likes your dad, right?"

"Most people like Abba."

"And you've got that program you're in. What's it called again?" Laurel scrunches up her brows.

"An individualized education plan." Or IEP for short. Dr. Talia says IEPs help schools accommodate kids like me to make sure I do well in my classes—it's also why I didn't get in trouble for missing Señor L's lecture. According to her, Lynnwood has a "robust" program for disabled students, which is a big reason why I go there.

"Yeah, that." Laurel scoots closer to me, hair swishing. "Have him ask Señor L for you. I bet Cody would like being on your team more anyway. Then we can hang out together, just like we planned."

"I've never seen Cody spend time with Andy or Gibs...."

Laurel shrugs. "They're all boys. They'd get along."

But Isa isn't.

My phone buzzes again, and I glance down.

Andy

Ellen! We saved you a seat at dinner.

Isa (they/them)

You slept more than Gibs

Andy

Which is impressive.

Gibs

Whatever, I need my beauty sleep u haters

"What do you think, Elle?"

I drag my gaze up to her, but don't say anything at first. None of my teammates seem mad at me about earlier. "I don't know...."

"Your dad said he wanted to give you space on this trip, right?"

"But I told him I didn't need it," I remind her.

"Just tell him you decided you want space after all. Pleeeease?" Laurel clasps her hands in front of her, eyes wide.

I duck my head but don't hide my smile. "Okay. I'll ask."

"Yay!" She flops onto my mattress. "This trip'll be *so* much better when we're together. When's the best time to ask your dad? Tomorrow at breakfast, maybe?"

My heart swells as I lie down beside her. Now I have another item to add to my list, because Laurel's excitement is contagious. "Tomorrow night might be better. Abba and I are going to call Mom before the group dinner."

"Good idea. We don't want other kids to overhear. Señor L might say no one can switch if lots of people ask." Still, Laurel frowns. "I just wish we didn't have to wait another whole day."

"Me neither. But at least it'll give me time to figure out what to say." The longer Laurel's idea is out there, the more my excitement builds. Abba won't say no to me. Then Laurel and I will get to spend the rest of the trip together, like we were supposed to.

"I can practice with you if you want help."

"You'd pretend to be Abba?" I side-eye her.

"Hey now, I could sound like your dad if I tried." She drops her voice. "The two Els, reunited at last."

Maybe I'm still tired, or slap-happy as Mrs. McKinley calls it, because I giggle. Laurel presses her lips together, but soon she's giggling with me. Our shoulders rise and fall together.

"Oh, also!" Laurel takes a moment to twist and face me. "I came up with the *best* story for this street artist I saw at Port Vell."

I settle in, hanging on to her every word as Laurel describes the performer.

One more day. I'll talk to Abba and then we'll have even more stories to tell each other. My world will rotate perfectly on-axis once more.

Chapter Thirteen

Day 3

I blink awake to a mostly dark room. A sliver of light divides it in two. It casts shadows on Laurel's face, but her eyes stay closed, breaths slow and steady.

I slide out of bed as quietly as I can, then tiptoe over to the window.

Directly across the courtyard, one window glows. A woman walks across her living space, then disappears out of view into another room. Three floors below, lamps light up the courtyard.

There's no point in going downstairs to call Mom again, not when we've already scheduled a call for tonight. Plus, she'd probably tell Abba I'm not sleeping.

I grab my phone and curl up in bed with my knees to my chest. Lowering my screen's brightness, I tap into my team's new group chat.

My teammates had a whole conversation while I napped yesterday. I scroll through it again, past the jokes about Gibs's snoring, to mentions of the first clue.

> **Andy**
> I did some research, and Gaudí built a ton of buildings in Barcelona
> **Isa (they/them)**
> Usually I stan an over-achiever, but ugh on this one… 😝
> **Andy**
> Yeah. But only two are on Passeig de Gràcia (aka el Paseo de Gracia): La Pedrera and Casa Battló. That shouldn't be too hard to narrow down
> **Isa (they/them)**
> For sure. Good thing Ellen is a genius and realized we were in the wrong place yesterday #teamwork
> **Andy**
> Yeah, totally!

Gibs joins in soon after, but I keep rereading the same section.

I still feel like I ruined things by insisting on going to La Sagrada Família.

Except Isa called me a genius and Andy agreed.

Hashtag teamwork.

I stare at both messages, reading them again and again, until my phone feels too heavy to hold up. Every thought scatters as I drift back to sleep.

In the morning, I enter the dining room with Laurel, Sophie-Anne, and Madison again. As I walk up the center aisle between tables, Abba waves at me from his seat between Mrs. West and Mrs. Delfina. I wave back, then spot Isa sitting across from Andy and Gibs.

A team of three. I'm the only one missing.

I pass by them fast, not stopping until I've grabbed a plate and filled it with food.

Meritxell sits farther up at the head of our table with Xavi today, plus a man and a woman who must be their parents. Their conversations mingle with those of my classmates. I try to catch a few words, but nothing she says sounds like the Spanish I learned in class.

"Hey, team."

I drag my eyes away from Meritxell and her family. Cody waves at us from across the table, then plops into his seat.

"And Ellen."

"Hi," I say back.

It's only then that I realize it's not just Andy, Gibs,

and Isa who're sitting together. Everyone else sits with their team, too.

"This stuff is way too strong." Madison doesn't bother to say hi to Cody as she sips her cup of coffee. "I would literally die for Starbucks right now."

"Same," Sophie-Anne chimes in at the same time Laurel says, "Me too."

I look at Laurel in surprise. She likes fruit-flavored teas, not coffee. Plus, no one is going to "literally die" without Starbucks. Not possible.

The dining room door opens, and Señor L enters.

"Another day, another dorky T-shirt." Madison laughs.

I glance back at Señor L, but he's already taken a seat with the other chaperones. All I see is a blue shirt with a few yellow letters. I doubt Laurel can see much more.

But she laughs, too. "Totally dorky."

Across from us, Cody folds his hands, then unfolds them, before swiveling in his seat to face the other table.

"Hey, I've got some great news," Laurel whispers, the moment Cody's back is turned. Sophie-Anne and Madison scoot closer. "Ellen's going to ask her dad to switch with Cody."

I cough as my juice goes down the wrong tube.

Sophie-Anne looks from me back to Laurel. "Oh my actual gosh, seriously?"

"Shh." Laurel points at Cody.

"Oops." Sophie-Anne lowers her voice. "That'd be awesome."

"You think he'll let her?" Madison asks.

"Probably," Laurel says. "Mr. Katz is really cool, like your mom with taking us to the beach yesterday."

"Mom's not cool," Madison says. "She just feels guilty about the divorce, so she says yes to everything I ask."

"So they'd really just switch Ellen with..." Sophie-Anne gestures to Cody's back.

Laurel grins. "Yep."

"Now *that* would be cool." Madison straightens back up.

They move on, talking about some cheerleading camp Madison and Sophie-Anne are attending in August. I tune them out and run through the script Laurel and I practiced last night. By the time I talk to Abba, I want to have it completely memorized.

"Hey, man." Jake Willaby leans toward Cody from the other table. "How's the hunt going?"

"Can't tell you." Cody shakes his hair out of his eyes. "It's against the rules, remember?"

"I know, I know. But there's nothing against the rules about saying my team is going to get done first. Emmaline's really good at Spanish, and Clara's in charge of all our navigating. We've definitely got this." Jake thrums his fingers against the back of his chair frame. It's erratic, not like the rhythm I use on my leg.

I don't catch Cody's response as my gaze snags on the team to his left. Sully's hunched next to Tess and her other teammates, taking notes on her clue sheet. Same for the rest of my team at the other table. Everyone's absorbed in the scavenger hunt except Laurel's team.

And me.

I keep my eyes on my plate and focus on eating until breakfast is over.

"Just one more day, Elle." Laurel crosses her fingers, and my stomach rolls. It's excitement. Or nerves. Maybe both.

As she heads out with her team, I walk over to Abba. "Boker tov, metukah."

"Boker tov." I follow him over to my teammates, repeating the greeting in English for them. "Morning."

"Hey," Andy says.

Gibs hops up from the table and gives me a quick wave.

As we exit the dining area, Isa pulls up beside me. "How're you feeling after yesterday?"

I choose my words carefully.

"Better." Which is true. "I'm sorry I didn't help you do research." Also true.

"All good," Isa says. "We decided to visit La Pedrera this morning."

"Which you would've known if you were sitting with us." Gibs gets to the front door first and slips through it.

It seems impossible for my face to feel any hotter in the dead heat of a Barcelona summer, but my cheeks burn at his comment. I remind myself this'll all be over after I talk to Abba later. They'll like having Cody as a teammate, and Cody will tell Jake about all the fun he's having and actually mean it.

"Gibs, shut up," Andy says.

"Yeah," Isa says. "Ellen can sit where she wants."

"I know she can," Gibs says. "But she's the *only* one not sitting with her team. That's kind of weird, don't you think?"

The others go quiet as we wait for the stoplight to turn. Yesterday's messages from Andy and Isa come back to me. They fight for space with the words Laurel helped me memorize for my talk with Abba tonight.

Good thing Ellen is a genius.

Hey, Abba, remember at the airport, when you told me you could give me space . . . ?

Hashtag teamwork.

That last one makes me feel a good kind of warm.

Except it doesn't even matter. Because after tonight, we won't be a team anymore.

Chapter Fourteen

We take the L4 metro line, following yellow signs today instead of blue. Two stops and we exit at Passeig de Gràcia.

My teammates chatter as we head back up to street level, but I stay quiet. If I don't get too involved now, maybe it'll be easier to make the switch tomorrow.

"Hey, y'all. Look!" Andy points toward the sidewalk.

We all crouch down, studying the hexagonal tiles. It's Gibs who snaps the first picture, but the rest of us aren't far behind. Each tile has a swirly design that connects to the other tiles on either side. I switch from taking photos to video, panning my phone from a close-up of the tiles to a longer view of the sidewalk.

"Did you guys see Señor L's shirt this morning?" Isa asks once we start walking again.

"Yeah." Andy grins.

"What was on it?" I ask, before remembering I wasn't going to talk to anyone.

"A palm tree with hands rising up out of it," Andy tells me. "It said *Las palmas arriba*."

He lifts his hands, and Isa copies him.

Gibs twists around to face us, walking backward. "Kinda nerdy if you ask me."

"We didn't." Isa throws him a too-wide smile that even I can tell is fake.

"That means..." Now that I've asked, I have to know the rest. "'Palms up'?"

Isa nods.

"I get the hands part, but what does the tree have to do with it?"

"Isn't it obvious?" Gibs asks.

"She wouldn't be asking if it was obvious to her," Isa says.

The warmth returns.

"It's a play on words," Andy explains. "The word *palma* sounds like *palm tree* in English. It means the palm of your hand in Spanish. But since we also know English, it's like an inside joke for people who understand both languages."

I think back to the shirt Señor L wore at the airport. "... Sort of like *llamas* in Spanish and *llamas* in English?

They're spelled the same but mean something completely different?"

All three of them nod. Even Gibs.

I hang back as we continue walking. Once everyone's in front of me, I allow my hands to flap. Just a little, and at my sides so it's less noticeable. Now I can't wait to see what Señor L wears tomorrow.

As we continue down the tile-lined sidewalk, Isa drops back to walk with me. "Did Andy's explanation make sense?"

"Yes. I don't know if I'll always get them," I admit, "but I understand the palmas and llamas ones now."

"I can come up with more examples," Isa says. "If something doesn't make sense, you could just ask me. Only if you want, though. If not, no big."

"Okay." I push away a twinge of guilt. "Thanks."

Ahead of us, a crowd waits in line outside a building.

"Pretty sure this is it," Andy says.

Isa takes it in. "It looks like..."

"...a hot mess," Gibs finishes.

For once, I agree with Gibs. La Pedrera looks like someone threw clay onto a building that dried before it could be smoothed out. It's the opposite of symmetrical.

Abba hands us tickets, and we enter through a black iron gate that looks all bent out of shape.

Gibs surges ahead. "Look!"

He points past the staircases on either side of us, to the building's interior walls. They're covered in earthy greens, oranges, reds, and golds.

"Pinturas murales," Isa murmurs, rolling perfect *r*'s in a way I've never been able to myself.

I pull out my phone, backing into the center of a sun-drenched courtyard as I record video. Squinting, I look up.

Windows rise in a spiral, all the way to the open sky. Light bounces off the panes of glass. A different type of sparkle from Sagrada Família, but the same type of mesmerizing.

Isa steps beside me. "Gaudí really liked to play with light in his designs, didn't he?"

Soon, all four of us are looking up, plus Abba.

The architect of light and silence. It fits. With all the other tourists here, it's not exactly quiet, but I can imagine how peaceful it'd be to sit by myself, letting the light wash over me.

"This is amazing," Andy says. "I never would've guessed the inside looked so cool."

I told myself not to get excited when we left the hotel. But surrounded by soft light and plants that gently sway from the ledge of a spiraling stone staircase, I want to flap again so badly.

I let a quick flick escape from my wrist, then another as we make our way to the stairs. My whole body feels light now. Totally relaxed. Andy leads, and I stay near the back of our group, filming the walls, the ceilings, everything.

"What do you think, metukah?"

I look over at Abba.

"It's..." I search for the right word. "Unique."

And different. Maybe Gaudí and I have something in common.

"I agree. Very different from back home, nachon?"

"Yes." I frown a little. "I wish Mom could see this."

"Me too," Abba says. "We'll have to come back with her someday."

We continue past the third-floor landing, up another spiraling set of steps.

"Speaking of your ima, are you excited to talk to her tonight?"

I nod, even though my chest tightens with nerves about what I'll be asking afterward.

On the fourth floor, we follow a tour group into an apartment that's set up like it's still the 1900s.

Andy snaps a picture of a fancy velvet couch, while Gibs studies an enormous old stove in the kitchen. In the bedroom, Isa takes a photo of lace curtains fluttering above an open window.

Room by room, I record with my phone. Every little detail.

Then it's up more stairs. Even though we're still inside, the space gets bigger and brighter the higher we climb. It feels like we're heading toward something special and exciting.

The next room we enter is lined with orange-red bricks, from the floor up to the ceiling arches.

"Hey, hey, hey." Gibs zips over to a detailed model of La Pedrera. "Attic museum."

I hold my breath as I look around, not wanting to get my hopes up again. Displays line the space. They hold architectural plans. Black-and-white photos. Even a documentary video playing from an iPad. I exhale, fingers tingling with relief as I study an old photo taken the year La Pedrera was built.

Street tiles: check

Wall paintings: present

And now we've found the attic museum.

Gibs is the first to disappear through the exit at the far end of the room, but Isa lingers by an exhibit. Sets of silver chains hang from the ceiling, like necklaces of different lengths. In the attic's dim light, they don't sparkle, but there's still something fascinating about them.

"Look." Isa waves me closer, then points to a mirror on the floor, directly underneath the chain model. "This is how Gaudí came up with the shapes for his building. Isn't it cool?"

I step forward, and the mirror reflects Gaudí's model in reverse. Now all the chains look like they're rising from the floor.

"It's unique." Also different. I've never seen anything like it.

My phone hovers under the chains, then over the mirror. My reflection peers back at me, my hair just a shade darker than the bricks on the ceiling.

"We should probably catch up with the others."

I look over at Isa, suddenly noticing we're the only ones still inside. The air shimmers with heat as we leave the cool building and step onto the roof. I blink in the bright sunlight.

"Warrior chimneys!" Nearby, Gibs points.

My eyes follow the line of his finger to one. Then another and another.

They're everywhere. Tall chimneys. Wide chimneys. Glass mosaics cover some, while others are carved out of off-white stone. Their tops look like helmets, the vents like narrowed eyes.

Birds soar through a clear blue sky overhead. A few swoop down and weave around the chimneys, like they've stopped their migration just to congratulate us. Beyond the roof, Barcelona apartments spread out in all directions, endless. A feeling of awe washes over me. I record everything.

"Hey, check it out!" Andy waves us over to a railing that looks down into the interior courtyard. He lifts his arms. From the building's smooth wall one floor below, shadow-Andy lifts his arms, too.

Isa waves their hands. Gibs creates a shadow giraffe with his fingers.

Before I can test it out, Isa sneaks behind Gibs and gives him rabbit ears.

"*Hey.*" He turns and swipes at them, but Isa jumps back, just in time for Andy to step in. The rabbit ears reappear on shadow-Gibs.

I giggle, and Gibs swats Andy's hand away.

"At least make me look cool. Give me antlers. Or a crown since I just solved the clue!"

"*We* just solved the clue," Isa says, but they spread their fingers above Gibs's head.

As Andy and Isa try to figure out how to make Gibs his crown, I lift my hand and study its shadow. I snap my thumb up to my other fingers, then release it, like a chomping mouth. It's not exactly the same tingly feeling as flicking my wrists, but I like the movement's repetition. I chomp again and again, making my way toward Gibs.

Isa notices me first. They laugh and join in, devouring Andy's side of the shadow-crown. Soon, Gibs is surrounded by chomping hands. By the time Abba appears, all four of us are laughing.

"How about you strike a pose?" Abba lifts his phone.

I raise one arm, and shadow-Ellen waves back.

Abba snaps a photo, then waits for us to pick a different pose. I lift my other arm, fingers spread as far as I can stretch them.

"Las palmas arriba." The words leave my mouth before I can stop myself.

"Totally." Andy raises his arms, fingers spread out just like mine. Soon Gibs and Isa lift their arms the same way.

"Got a good one!" Abba calls.

"BAM." Gibs lifts his arms again. He aims his phone at one of the chimneys and snaps a picture. "We nailed this one. Watch out, clue two! We're coming for you."

Andy nods. "Let's talk to Señor L before the group dinner tonight to get the next clue."

"I can't," I say fast. "My dad and I are supposed to call my mom then."

"We could just talk to Señor L after his lecture," Gibs says.

"We could..." Andy presses his lips together. "But then other teams might overhear."

"The instructions didn't say that we all have to talk to Señor L, right?" Isa asks Andy.

"Nope. Just that we have to solve the first clue before he'll give us the second. We can do clue one just the three of us."

This could be good for all of us, I realize. By the time they get the second clue, I'll already have talked to Abba about switching teams.

"Cool. And then Ellen can be there for the others." Isa turns to me. "If that's okay with you?"

I chew on the inside of my cheek and nod.

"Teamwork for the win!" Gibs shouts into the courtyard. Four floors down, tourists blink up at us.

He takes off toward a bridge that leads to another part of the roof, with Andy close behind. Isa stays by the interior railing, and I drift toward the roof's outer edge, occasionally pausing to start a new video clip.

Teamwork. One clue down, two to go. A breeze whips my hair around my face, cool and salty. I flap my free hand, away from my teammates.

I go still as my eyes follow a tour bus down a street that divides two long rows of apartment buildings. The roads on either side of it all seem to lead to the same place, just out of sight in the distance.

"Yo, Ellen!" I turn, spotting Gibs and the rest of my group near the roof exit. "Ready to go?"

I take one last look out across the city, then head downstairs with everyone.

We stop in a gift shop on our way out. Gibs and Andy head toward a display of figurines, and Isa sorts through Gaudí-themed T-shirts. I wander over to a rack of post-cards and spin through images of famous Barcelona sites, only some of which I recognize. One is an image with the sidewalk tiles. I study it, then twirl the rack again.

Another catches my eye. It's Barcelona at dusk, with a quotation in the center. I slide it out.

TOMORROW WE WILL DO BEAUTIFUL THINGS.
—A. GAUDÍ

I read it again. Last year, my English teacher told us to be specific whenever we write essays. Vague words aren't as good as saying exactly what you mean. Gaudí didn't have Ms. Allen for English, so he probably didn't know this.

Isa steps beside me, a set of Gaudí tile coasters in one hand. "I think I'm going to get these for my parents."

Nearby, Andy stands next to Gibs, who slides a color-ful figurine toward the cashier.

"This guy is so cool," Gibs says. "He reminds me of my pet lizard back home."

"It is a replica of a full-size statue in Park Güell," the cashier says. "Have you seen it yet?"

"Uh, no? But that sounds awesome." Gibs turns to

Andy. "We're going to that park, even if it's not part of the scavenger hunt. Sorry, I don't make the rules."

Andy looks up at the cashier. "Is it close by?"

"Three kilometers away. Maybe four. It is on a hill."

"So not something we can just walk to," Andy says. "But we can map out directions back at the hotel and figure out the best day to visit."

That's an adventure I won't be around for.

Isa eyes the postcard in my hands. "Are you going to buy that?"

I think of my neglected dot diary. If we were still on our old schedule, I'd know what we'd be doing tomorrow and whether it could be beautiful. Until I can talk to Abba about switching teams tonight, everything feels off-axis. Uncertain.

"No, just looking." I put the postcard back on the rack and follow Isa to the cash register.

Chapter Fifteen

After our siesta, I hop out of bed and grab my room key.

"Is it time?" Laurel asks.

I nod.

"*Finally.*" She bounces on her bed. "Good luck!"

My chest flutters with excitement and nerves as I say goodbye to her. I close the door, then spot a sheet of paper taped to it. It's a pencil sketch of La Pedrera. Abba's drawn four shadows looking up toward the roof, where each of my teammates poses.

Across the hall, Isa's door has a sketch taped to it as well. It's us in the subway, Isa leading the way.

I take the La Pedrera sketch, stomach alive with jitters.

Upstairs, I knock on room 3B's door.

"It's unlocked," Abba calls.

He spots the drawing in my hands as I enter. "I didn't feel like napping. Do you like it?"

"Yes. Did you draw something for Andy and Gibs, too?"

"I did." Abba gestures to his bed. His room is like mine except there's only one of everything, plus a desk where Abba currently sits. "I sketched a little something for each member of your team."

Nerves swirl in my stomach as Abba unlocks his iPad. Abba clicks into Mom's contact info, and I silently repeat the first words of the script Laurel and I came up with.

Remember when you told me you could give me space at the airport, but I said I didn't need it? I was wrong. . . .

I thrum my fingers as Mom's face fills the screen.

"Hello, hello!" Mom lifts a piece of fabric up to the screen. "Look who found a new hobby."

"Is that . . ." Abba's brows scrunch. "A cactus?"

"It is!" Mom beams. "I'm learning to cross-stitch. I should have all ten cacti in this pattern done by the time you get back."

"What happened to learning Southern phrases?" I ask.

"Oh, I was as lost as last year's Easter egg trying to keep them straight." Mom laughs. "Cross-stitch makes so much more sense to me. It's also relaxing. Anyway, how are my favorite people?"

Abba looks at me. "I don't know about Ellen, but I'm zonked."

"Because he was drawing instead of napping this afternoon." I hold up the sketch.

"Traitor!" Abba winks. That's my cue to know he's joking.

"I see." Mom leans in, and I move the sketch closer to the screen. "Is that your scavenger hunt team?"

Not for long.

"Yes." My shoulders tense, even though it's technically not a lie yet.

"You all look so happy. Now tell me, where have you visited so far?"

Relief washes through me when she doesn't ask more questions about my teammates. I tell her about La Sagrada Família, then La Pedrera.

"You know," Mom says, "I took a few art history classes in undergrad, back before I decided to become a cantor. Gaudí has such an unusual style. Barcelona also has a gorgeous Gothic Quarter, and probably some of the best—"

"Miriam," Abba says. "Let's leave it for Ellen to discover."

"Oh, of course, of course. I'm just thrilled you're having so much fun."

With a jolt, I realize I am. I like being a part of my team.

Abba asks Mom about her workday, but I tune them out and try to imagine being on a team with Laurel, Sophie-Anne, and Madison. Like *really* imagine us figuring out clues and exploring places.

I can't.

But it's what I want, isn't it?

Mom's phone rings, pulling me out of my thoughts.

"It's the temple," she says. "Ugh, I have to take this. But I promise we'll talk again soon."

"Right before Shabbat?" I ask.

"Absolutely."

We say our goodbyes. The screen goes dark, and Abba switches over to his email account.

"Well, that was a nice talk with your ima, even though it got cut short."

"Yes." I swallow. "Abba?"

"Hmm?" His eyes stay on his iPad, skimming a new email.

My phone vibrates in my pocket before I can say anything. Three private chat messages from Isa.

Isa (they/them)

As promised, all the puns I could think of.

Isa (they/them)

Let me know if you need help figuring any out!

Isa (they/them)

No matter how hard you push the envelope, it's still stationery ✉️

Time flies like an arrow ⏱️ Fruit flies like a banana 🍌

You can tune a piano but you can't tuna fish 🎵🐟

The list goes on. So many lines to dissect.

The warm feeling returns. I close my eyes, savoring it.

"Did you need something, metukah?"

I startle, eyes flying open. "No."

Wait, I did, though.

Abba looks at me. "You're sure?"

This is my chance. All I have to do is recite my script.

But I'm still stuck on Isa and their pun list. I shake my head.

I take the stairs back to my room as slowly as I can, trying to figure out what happened before I have to face Laurel.

Maybe I didn't want to hurt my teammates' feelings.

Or maybe I didn't ask because it wouldn't be fair to change teams after we already solved la primera pista.

I still don't have a clue by the time I spot Laurel in

the hall outside our hotel room. She's put on makeup since I left and changed into a pale-orange dress.

"I couldn't wait for you to get back." She looks at Abba's sketch in my hands. "This is so cute. I just wish he'd drawn you as part of our team." She doesn't seem to notice my silence. "So, what did your dad—"

A door opens. Isa steps out into the hall.

"Hey." They look at Laurel, then over to me. "Did you get my chat messages?"

I nod, throat tight.

"Cool. Also, Señor L liked how we solved the first clue. He gave us copies of la segunda pista."

"Oh, good."

Isa passes me a sheet of paper. I fold it small enough to fit in my pocket as my throat gets tighter.

Laurel's eyes are on me, but another door opens before I can speak. Boys appear on the stairway. Soon, everyone's making their way downstairs.

As Señor L leads us to a nearby restaurant, I find myself sandwiched between two very different groups. To my right, Laurel walks beside me, with Sophie-Anne and Madison, all in dresses. On my left, my actual team-mates wear shorts and T-shirts.

"Did you guys get a drawing from Mr. Katz, too?" Isa asks.

"Yeah!" Gibs's voice rings in my ears. "Mine was of all of us at the church."

"What kind of food do they eat in Barcelona?" Sophie-Anne asks Madison. "I mean, besides what we've been eating at the hotel."

"He's seriously good at drawing." That's probably Isa, but it's hard to tell. No one else seems to have problems hearing their friends when people talk over one another. Just me.

"Lots of seafood," Madison says.

"He's actually a professional artist." Andy this time. "Have you read his graphic novels?"

I don't get a chance to hear Isa's response before Laurel takes my hand and pulls me toward an empty table at the edge of the outdoor seating area. The adults take the table next to us, then my teammates sit down one more spot over. A mix of voices reaches me from Abba's table, then laughter from Andy, Isa, and Gibs.

I should be chatting with them.

"So." Laurel taps my shoulder. "What'd your dad say?"

Sophie-Anne and Madison lean forward.

Before I can respond, a server appears. She hands us menus. "¿Bebidas?"

While Madison and Laurel both order a Coke, I pick at the edge of my black shorts.

"Agua, por favor," Sophie-Anne says.

"¿Agua con gas o sin gas?" the server asks her.

"Sorry, what?"

"Still or sparkling water."

"Oh. Sparkling, please!"

I order, too. The server leaves us menus, then everyone's eyes return to me.

"I"—my throat still feels thick, but I force the words out—"can't be on your team."

I take a shallow breath, preparing to defend my decision.

"He said no?" Laurel frowns.

I shake my head—as in, Abba didn't say no because I chose not to ask him.

"I figured that'd happen." Madison reaches for a menu.

"Still sucks, though." Sophie-Anne leans toward Madison to read over her shoulder.

"It really sucks." Laurel's shoulders slump. "I'm sorry you're stuck on that team, Elle."

Before I can form the words to correct Laurel, Madison sighs.

"And *I'm* sorry we're stuck with Cody. He stinks. As in, literally needs better deodorant."

I don't remember Cody smelling when he sat across from us this morning, but Madison doesn't linger on the

subject as she scans her menu. "Anyway, we should figure out what we want to eat. I think the paella."

Two teen girls pass us on the sidewalk. One holds
a phone in front of them both, as they video chat with
someone in Spanish. I want to nudge Laurel so we can
come up with their story.

Except Laurel's huddled over Madison's menu.

Nearby, Jake brags that his team's done with two
clues already. Gibs says something back that I can't quite
make out, then laughter erupts from both tables.

Even though I'm sitting with Laurel, it feels like I'm
sandwiched between two groups of people, still the odd
one out.

SEGUNDA PISTA

Para los que me visitan

soy una calle

muy grande y famosa.

❧

Busquen los artistos callejeros

y un mosaico

amarillo, azul y rojo

en dirección a la playa.

❧

¡Buena suerte otra vez!

Chapter Sixteen

Day 4

The next morning, my eyes flutter open much earlier than they should.

Not again.

For a few minutes, I lie in bed, trying to fall back to sleep. But the *tick-tick-tick* of the wall clock and air conditioner's steady hum combine forces. The thin strip of light feels like a barrier this morning, separating me from Laurel. I slide out of bed to close the curtains.

Mist blankets the courtyard below, making the lamplights look hazy. I shiver, then reach up to move the curtain.

The tall grass sways, then goes still. I stare for so long, I start to wonder if I imagined it.

Someone else appears, right below my window. Dark purple hair. The glint of a silver stud in one ear. I watch

Isa wade through the grass, then disappear behind a toolshed.

Now I'm positive I won't be able to go back to sleep.

I put on shoes, and grab my phone and room key, then head out.

On the ground floor, I make my way toward the far end of the hall. I pause in front of the door that Meritxell came out of when my team ran into her on Monday. Meritxell and her smile that makes my chest flutter. Meritxell, who makes it seem so simple to say exactly what you're thinking.

I couldn't even manage to tell Laurel what actually happened with Abba yesterday.

At the end of the hall, a door is cracked open a sliver. I slip outside and wade toward the center of the court-yard, just like Isa did a few minutes ago. Now that I'm down here, it reminds me more of an overgrown garden.

Voices. Soft, whispered words.

I inch closer to the shed.

A small clearing appears on the other side of the shed, framed by benches. Isa's perched on one, Andy another.

Isa spots me first.

"Ellen, hey." Once again, a single earbud cord snakes out of Isa's ear.

"Hi. What are you doing down here?"

"Couldn't sleep," Andy says. "Gibs's snoring is epic. I should record it for y'all sometime."

I glance over at Isa. "What about you?"

"I've just always liked being up late at night. Back home, it's the only time my house is quiet." They shrug. "Want to sit with us?"

Isa points to an empty bench between the two of them.

"Does Laurel snore, too?" Isa asks once I'm seated.

"No. I just couldn't sleep."

I keep my eyes on the ground. A light breeze rustles shoots of grass that stick up from cracks in the cement.

"Gotcha." Out of the corner of my eye, I spot Isa crossing one leg over the other. "Andy was just about to show me one of your dad's graphic novels."

"Yeah!" Andy pulls the Fisher omnibus out of his bag. It's a special edition that features all three volumes of Abba's latest series.

He hands it over to Isa, who studies the cover. "His art is incredible. Like, seriously amazing."

"It's awesome, yeah," Andy says. "And the story is beyond epic. It's set in the South but it's an alternate universe where each town has a different Paradigm. Actually . . ." He turns to me. "Ellen can probably explain it better."

My eyes dart up to Andy, then down again. For once, I'm not wishing Laurel would step in. She's never read Abba's novels.

I take a breath.

"It's a set of rules that everyone in each town has to follow." The Paradigms are my favorite part because they remind me of my dot diary categories: straightforward and logical.

"Right." Andy leans forward. "So, volume one is about a boy, Fisher, and how he starts questioning his town's Paradigm. By volume three, he and his friends are trying to take down the entire system."

Isa flips through the pages. "Yeah, I'll definitely be reading this. Cool if I borrow it?"

"Sure," Andy says. "There's a character named Comet who's my favorite. Plus, no one really dates anyone, so the fandom can ship each character with whoever they want."

Just like Abba chose specific terms for the Paradigm rule system, I know there are special words in the world of graphic novel readers. *Fandom* is a group of people who all like the same thing: graphic novels, obviously, but also TV shows, video games, and other stuff. Then *ship* is short for *relationship*, except it's a verb.

I glance at Andy. "Do you ship Comet with anyone?"

"I, um. Kind of." Andy's hands tighten their grip on the edge of his bench.

Did I say something wrong?

"Hey . . ." Isa looks up. "Can you wait until I have a chance to read? Then I can tell you who I ship, too."

"Yeah, totally." Andy's hands relax.

There are plenty of characters in *Fisher's Final*, but I've never really thought about shipping any of them. My thoughts flicker to Meritxell, then back to Abba's novels. I wonder if any of the girl characters might be good together.

"So, has anyone looked at the second clue yet?" Isa asks.

Andy and I both shake our heads.

"Want to see if we can figure it out?"

"Sure." Andy reaches for his phone and backpack.

I glance between them as Isa also pulls out their clue. "I didn't bring it with."

I didn't even remember to look at it after dinner. It's still folded up in my shorts pocket.

"That's okay," Isa says. "You can look at mine."

Isa scoots to the edge of their bench. I steal a glance at their earbud as I take a seat. If they have anything playing, it's too soft to hear.

"Just so you know," Andy tells me, "getting Señor L to approve our first clue yesterday wasn't too hard."

"Yeah." Isa holds their clue sheet out for me. "He just asked us to choose who was going to recite it in Spanish, then translate it and show him some pics of where we went. Andy volunteered."

"Oh, okay." That doesn't sound too bad, but the

thought of reciting Spanish in front of my classmates twists my stomach. As Andy hunches over his phone, I study Isa's clue sheet. Maybe I can convince Isa and Gibs to recite the other clues if I do a good job helping to solve them.

Isa's translated a few words that already appeared in clue one (*calle*, *busquen*) and others that I remember learning in class last year (*visitan*, *grande*, *playa*, plus all three mosaic colors).

Two words catch my attention. Isa's written @ signs over both *o*'s in "artist@s callejer@s."

"What're those for?"

"Nothing clue-related. I just made them gender neutral."

"Like the Spanish version of *they*, *their*, and *them*?"

"Sorta. You know how words that describe women usually end in -*as*, and for men it's -*os*?"

"Yes." I learned this in Spanish last year.

"Well, the @ sign with an *s* at the end is the gender-neutral version you can use for nonbinary people, or just groups in general. Some people use an *x* instead— like they'd say *Latinx* instead of *Latino* or *Latina*—but I think the @ sign is more fun to write."

I consider this. "So, if you needed to put something like this into categories, it could be 'men,' 'women,' and . . . 'nonbinary'?"

"Yep," Isa says. " 'Other' could work, too. Or 'gender neutral.' "

Excitement surges through me. It makes sense when Isa explains it like this. Now I have a new dot diary list to put under my pronouns category.

"Okay! I think I've got it translated." Isa and I look over at Andy, who sits up straighter on his bench. "There's no confusing stuff like warrior chimneys this time, so that made it easier. It looks like we've just got to find a big, famous street that has street performers, a mosaic, and a beach."

"That's"—Isa squints at their clue sheet—"not very specific."

A memory sparks. Something about Laurel. Possibly shopping?

"Yeah," Andy says. "There are tons of places where you can see these things, I bet."

Isa and I reach for our phones at the same time.

"There are *so many* streets that lead to the beach." Isa stares at a Google map, shoulders rounded. "Not sure they'd all have performers and a yellow, blue, and red mosaic, but yeah."

I flip through my videos until I get to the one I took at La Pedrera, panning across apartment rooftops. I pause it at the street where double-decker buses seemed to be dropping off tourists.

Isa leans closer to me. "Did you find something?"

I click off my phone fast. My videos feel private.

"Maybe."

La Sagrada Família felt right, too, and I don't want to be wrong twice.

"What've you got?" Now Andy looks at me, too.

What did Laurel call that place Madison told her about? I should've written it down.

"Laurel said there's a huge street that has lots of shopping on it, plus street performers. It also leads to the beach."

Isa sits up. "That could be it."

"Except I don't remember what it was called."

"Top ten...famous...streets...Barcelona." Andy types into his phone. "Okay, there's Avinguda Diagonal."

I shake my head.

"Passeig de Gràcia," Andy says next. "But Señor L wouldn't have us go to the same place twice."

He looks back down at his phone. "How about Carrer Petritxol? Rambla de Ravel?"

"That one!" I say. "But just the 'rambla' part."

Andy's fingers fly over his phone screen again. "*Rambla* means 'boulevard,' but there's a famous one that's just called La Rambla." His voice rises in excitement. "It starts at a big square called Plaça de Catalunya and goes all the way to the Mediterranean Sea. Does that sound right?"

"Yes." I don't let myself get as excited as Andy yet. "That might not be what the clue means, though."

"Sure. But at least it gives us a place to explore tomorrow." Isa yawns.

Andy yawns, too, and I yawn along with him.

"La Rambla it is, then?" Isa stands.

"After a couple more hours of rest," Andy says.

"Well, obviously!" They shoot him a grin.

One by one, we wade through the weedy grass.

As we reach the steps that lead up into the hotel, I look at them both. "Will Gibs be mad that we worked on the clue without him?"

"No way." Andy shakes his head. "He'll probably be glad we already figured it out, to be honest. Doing homework isn't his favorite thing in the world."

"That *totally* sounds like Gibs," Isa says.

We head inside, then say goodbye to Andy on the girls-plus-Isa floor landing.

"Hope you can get a little more sleep," Isa whispers to me. "But if you ever wake up early again, now you have someplace to hang out with me. Andy too."

I return to bed with happiness warming my chest.

Chapter Seventeen

Buildings tower over a square framed by tour buses as we exit the subway station. Sunlight sparkles off water flowing from fountains.

"This feels like Times Square, except without all the billboards," Isa tells us, and I agree. Plaça de Catalunya has the same type of energy. Everywhere I turn is teeming with tourists. It's hard to know where to look.

Vendors shout at us. One blows a noisemaker that sounds like the high-pitched chirps of a bird, and I clench my jaw. I want to slip on my headphones to drown out the sounds, but I resist the urge.

I keep my phone out, videoing as we walk toward La Rambla across the street. We wait for the light to turn at a crowded curb. Cars honk, and bus brakes squeal. Tourists shout and call out to one another. My teammates aren't talking right now, but I doubt I'd be able to hear them even if they were.

Just like the pedestrian avenue by our hotel, La Rambla is wide, with narrower traffic lanes on both sides. That's where the similarity ends. Shopping bag handles hang like bracelets from people's arms. Spanish is just one of the languages I hear as tourists flood past us.

"Whoa, cool!" Gibs tears off, toward a man who looks like he's floating in thin air. I follow Gibs with my phone as he crouches, trying to figure out the illusion. He drops coins into a donation cup, then darts over to the next performer.

Nearby, Andy studies a man dressed entirely in silver who stands on a tiny platform, still as a statue.

"Hey, look." Isa points to the opposite side of the boulevard. "That performer's dressed as Jack Skellington."

"*The Nightmare Before Christmas* is another favorite movie of ours," Abba says. "Right, Ellen?"

I nod. At least I think I do. A pair of women flap butterfly wings in the corner of my vision, and my gaze sticks to them.

Gibs returns, then runs off again, tossing a coin into one of the butterfly women's cups.

My ears ring long after it's settled at the bottom.

The crowd gets thicker as we walk. I press my arms to my sides, trying to avoid brushing up against anyone.

My teammates wade through the crush of tourists, toward a crosswalk. La Rambla feels smaller and tighter by the second.

"Look." Andy's voice echoes like he's at the opposite end of a hallway.

I force my gaze up to a sign across the street, framed by colorful mosaic glass:

MERCAT
ST JOSEP
LA BOQUERÍA

Beneath it, throngs of people bump into one another as they enter the cramped space. My stomach swirls, vision blurring in and out of focus, as the streetlight changes.

My teammates start to cross the road, but I can't move an inch.

Sunlight flashes off building windows
people's sunglasses
the screens of their phones.

Sounds roar like a music scale
sung three octaves too high
completely off-tune.

Every touch
pricks like a needle
as people stream past me.

Ahead, Abba pauses. Looks around. Says something to Andy, Gibs, Isa.

They turn back.

"Hakol beseder, metukah?"

I squeeze my eyes shut.

Can't even shake my head in response.

Too much, too much.

"Mah at tsarichah?" His voice is quiet, words only for me.

What do I need?

I need...

...to cry.

No, *shriek*.

To rock and flail my arms until people stay away from me.

My pulse races. Muscles rigid, my whole body aches with tension.

My teammates' voices warp.

"Is she okay?" That's Isa. They, them, their. Non-binary. Other.

"We can skip—" A flash of brown hair. Gibs? "Not hungry right now anyway."

"Is there—" I flinch away from Andy's voice.

"—do for you, Ellen?" Quieter now. Still too loud.

Abba's next. But his words don't make sense. Can't process.

149

Hands slide into both of mine, one big and strong, the other smaller. Abba's grip is firm. Isa squeezes, then releases, then squeezes again. Their touch stings as I blink in the too-bright light. But I hold on tight as they lead me away from the crowd.

Across the street. Down a smaller road. I squeeze my eyes shut.

The noise suddenly stops. For a moment, it feels like my world has paused.

I suck in a breath of cool air, then let go of Abba and Isa. No more pain or too-bright lights. Sounds return to a normal volume. I wrap my arms around myself in the corner of this small shop.

"What was that?" Gibs asks. "Like, I know you're autistic, but what happened?"

I clench my jaw, waiting for Andy to say something or elbow Gibs.

He does neither.

"Maybe it's none of your business," Isa says, but their voice is hesitant, like a question.

"I—" There's a weight in my throat, anchoring my words. I look to Abba, but he stays quiet. It's my choice to share.

Or not.

"I can't go back out there," I finally manage.

I wait for Gibs to complain, to say we're wasting time

or to point out that, *hello*, I didn't actually answer his question.

But it's Isa who speaks first. "It's not like we're in a rush. Is everyone cool with staying here and looking around?"

Relief floods through me when Andy and Gibs nod.

My teammates wander off, browsing shelves throughout the shop.

Abba stays close. Not saying anything, just there if I need him. I focus on my breaths, on each deep inhale, then release of air. My pulse slows. Colors look normal, shapes crisp again.

"I'm okay now," I tell Abba.

"Okay, metukah," he says. "We'll stay here as long as you need."

I glance around the shop, expecting souvenirs like there were at La Pedrera—and there are some, along the walls. But the center of the shop mostly displays tiles.

As Abba joins Andy and Gibs over by a keychain stand, I take a step closer to a large center table. Relief mixes with embarrassment that my teammates saw me get so overwhelmed. I need a moment to myself.

Most of the tiles are painted in shiny, shimmery colors. A few look like copies of the Gaudí tiles on Passeig de Gràcia. Six-sided, with a swirl of design.

"I kind of wish I'd waited on buying those coasters."

Isa steps beside me, voice low. "These look a lot more like the real thing."

Eyes on the tiles, I don't respond. Whenever I go quiet, Laurel fills the silence with talk of gymnastics, school, or whatever's on her mind. Isa just reaches out to examine a tile with a cat painted on it.

Body still tense, I glance toward Andy and Gibs. Maybe they don't know exactly what being autistic means, but they've at least gone to school with me for years. Isa hasn't.

"Sometimes..." I hug myself tighter as Isa turns to me. "I mean, have you ever piled more things in your arms than you can easily hold?"

"Sure. One of my chores is to do the laundry."

"That's a little like how it feels. The heat and noise and light and people bumping into me are like different clothes I'm trying to hold on to. And if one more thing gets added, everything could topple."

"Then you have to slow down so things don't drop? Or find someone to help you carry something, maybe?"

"Yes." I lower my arms to my sides. "I don't know how to compare this part to laundry, but sometimes I have to focus so much on the other stuff that I can't tell when someone's talking to me. And sometimes I know they are, but I can't understand what they're saying."

I hold my breath as Isa turns a flower tile over in their hands. "So, definitely telling my sibs to be quiet when you come over to hang out."

The tension drains out of me as I exhale. Isa sets the tile down and waves me toward a stack of folded T-shirts.

"Is there any way to stop it before it starts?" Isa asks. "The toppling part?"

"Not always." I chew on the inside of my cheek. "But . . . these work sometimes."

I slide my backpack off my shoulders and show Isa my headphones. "I didn't want you all to get mad, thinking I was ignoring you, though."

"Not a chance." Isa shakes their head. "We'd understand. And if Gibs was being Gibs, I'd just tell him to shut it."

A smile tugs at the corners of my mouth. "Or Andy could elbow him."

"Or that." Isa laughs. They unfold a T-shirt, then hold it in front of themself. "What do you think?"

It has a graphic of the Barcelona metro map. The fabric looks soft, the size big enough not to pinch under the arms.

"I like it." I study its collar. "If the neck is too scratchy, I can show you how to remove the tag without tearing anything."

"Legit." Isa grins.

"Hey," Gibs calls. "We're pretty much done. Meet you outside?"

My hands don't quite flap at my sides as we make our way up to the cash register, but I allow my fingers to flutter. I glance toward a small display of postcards as Isa hands over some euros to the cashier.

My fingers go still. "My owl."

"Your what?" Isa looks over, and I pass the postcard to them. "Wow. Our hotel is famous. Are you going to get it?"

"Yes." My gaze drifts back to the rack as I slide the owl postcard to the cashier. A photo of Barcelona at dusk looks back.

Beautiful things. Tomorrow. Gaudí.

The quote still seems too vague. But something also feels different now.

"Wait," I tell the cashier, then grab the second postcard. "I'll also get this one."

Port Vell overflows with people: shoppers, street artists, beachgoers, but this time I'm prepared. I keep a hand on my headphones as we choose a café with outdoor seating that's quieter but still close enough to people-watch. A server takes our drink orders, then hands us menus.

I try to keep my focus on my teammates and our

table. We made it here by taking less crowded side streets. Occasionally, I'd catch glimpses of La Rambla in the distance and my arms would tingle with relief to be someplace quieter.

But a thought still nags me.

"We missed the mosaic," I say, sliding my headphones to my shoulders. "If there even was one."

"Gibs and I actually talked about that while you were in the shop," Andy says. "We probably don't have time to look for it today before Señor L's lecture, but we can just come back tomorrow morning and complete the clue."

"Yep." Gibs points his newest souvenir at Andy. It's the same brightly colored lizard that he got at La Pedrera, except a stuffed animal this time. "Then we'll have plenty of time to figure out clue three."

Andy looks at Isa and me from across the table. "If that's okay with y'all."

"Cool."

"Yes."

Isa and I answer at the same time.

"Jinx!" Isa grins.

I look down at my menu, cheeks filling with heat.

"So, what're tapas, exactly?" Gibs studies his menu, too.

"They're just small dishes, I think," Andy says. "Sort of like appetizers."

"We could order a bunch of them and share," Isa suggests.

"Just no pork for me or Abba," I say. "Or shellfish."

"That's like half the menu." Gibs groans.

"It does look that way," Abba says, eyes on his menu. "Seems like a perfect time for an NK day, don't you think, Ellen?"

He looks up, then winks at me to show me he's joking.

"What's an NK day?" Isa looks between us.

"It means 'non-kosher,'" I say. "Some Jewish people have them so they can eat food they're not supposed to. But not us. Right, Abba?"

"Mm." Abba just smiles, then looks back down at his menu.

"So it's probably easiest for you to just order stuff that doesn't have meat in it? Just to be safe?" Isa looks at me, and I nod. "I'm good with that, too, if you and Mr. Katz are cool sharing with me."

"Then Gibs and I can order some of the other tapas," Andy says.

"*Perfect*." Gibs lifts his lizard over his head like a trophy. A tag hangs off of its scaly, ridged back, glinting in the sun.

Once we place our order with the server, Gibs clears his throat.

"I have an important announcement." We all look at

156

him, and he flicks the stuffed animal's tag. "According to this, my lizard has a name: El Drac."

"What's it mean?" Andy asks.

"Who knows?" Gibs shrugs. "But that's what he should be called from here on out."

"I hope you know you're a total weirdo," Isa tells him.

"A weirdo who now owns a very cool lizard stuffed animal."

As Gibs and Isa keep going back and forth, I pull out my phone. This time, I feel calm enough to pay attention while I video the seating area, people walking past, and the port in the distance. I twist in my seat to get a shot of the café, pausing on a sign taped to its window.

It's all primary and secondary colors, just like the rainbow stickers on Abba's iPad.

I glance at my teammates, but they're still chattering. The server returns with our food, and I put my phone away.

We separate our plates by meat and vegetarian, then all dig in.

Eventually, Abba looks up. "Mr. Andy, Mr. Gibs: How's your food?"

Mouth still full, Andy nods. Gibs pinches his fingers together and lifts them to his face. "Chef's kiss, Señor Katz." He glances over at our plates. "Although that one looks awesome, too. What is it?"

"I think it was called patatas bravas," Isa says. "It's just potatoes with a creamy sauce."

"Can I try some?" Gibs's eyes never leave our plate.

"We will take your request under consideration," Isa says. "Right, Ellen?"

Even though Isa didn't wink, this feels like a joke to me.

"Yes," I play along. "We will get back to you within five business days."

"Wait, what?" Gibs finally looks up from the patatas.

Isa's grin gives us away.

"Oh, dang." Gibs shakes his head. "I walked right into that, huh?"

"Yes," I confirm.

Across the table, Andy snorts.

Soon, we're all laughing. Even Gibs.

Chapter Eighteen

Day 5

I set my alarm for 4:00 a.m. on Thursday morning.

The door to the garden isn't propped open tonight, so I twist the deadbolt on my own, then head outside.

I take a seat and pull out my dot diary while I wait. I've tried to keep it as updated as possible, but it's become more of a record of where I've visited than a schedule of future events.

I check my phone.

4:06 a.m.

Suddenly, my world tilts. What if Andy and Isa don't come? What if they picked a different place to hang out and didn't tell me?

I set my diary down and wrap my arms around myself. I rock, but my thoughts still spiral.

On day one, I messed up la primera pista. Then

yesterday didn't go as planned. Also my fault. Maybe my teammates are annoyed we didn't finish la segunda pista and decided not to show up.

I rock faster, but the worry doesn't go away.

A flash of movement slows me. My eyes dart to the back door. Isa appears, then Andy.

"You beat us today," Isa whispers.

I move my diary to my lap so Isa can sit beside me. Andy claims the bench across from us.

"I thought you weren't coming," I admit.

Isa blows air between their lips in a way that Laurel calls a raspberry. "We would've told you at dinner if we weren't going to come."

"Or texted," Andy chimes in.

Their words melt away some of my tension.

"I did some research after dinner last night," I say. It was when Laurel and I were supposed to catch up, but she was one room over with Sophie-Anne and Madison, painting their nails. She invited me to join, but just the thought of sharp nail polish smell was enough to say no. "There's a big mosaic on La Rambla that has all the colors on the pista. It's called Pla de l'Os."

Isa repeats the words as slowly as I spoke them. "That doesn't sound like Spanish."

"It's not, I don't think." I shake my head. "Remember

Señor L's lecture yesterday? When he said this whole region is called Catalunya?"

Isa and Andy nod.

"I looked up more about it, and lots of people here speak a language called Catalan."

Catalan might actually be what Meritxell and her family are speaking whenever their accents don't sound like Spanish to me.

"That's really cool," Andy says. "So that mosaic should be the first place we visit after breakfast."

Isa turns to me. "Want to add it to your bullet journal?"

My cheeks flush before I can look down.

"Sorry, was I not supposed to know about it?" Isa asks. "I just noticed you had it in the airport and a few other places."

"It's okay." I shake my head. "It wasn't a secret."

I open my diary and get to work as Isa pops in an earbud. Across from us, Andy scrolls through notifications on his phone, but I barely notice. There are a lot of things I need to update. Canceled events. Afternoon instead of morning field trips and lectures. I haven't even written any daily recaps.

"Okay, so, Isa..." I don't look up when Andy speaks next. "I talked to him. Again, I mean. We already talked once when I asked about subway directions, obviously."

"Obviously."

I hunch closer to my diary, trying to focus, but I can't help listening as Isa continues.

"And? Come on, the suspense is killing me."

"Well...we just talked about La Rambla. Basic stuff since my Spanish isn't that great, you know? But when I told him we didn't get a chance to visit the boquería, he said there's one near the hotel. It's smaller, but we could totally get lunch there sometime."

"I hope you invited him to come," Isa says.

I turn to an empty page but don't write anything.

"I forgot." I steal a glance at Andy, who's wringing his hands in his lap. "Okay, I actually wussed out. Because there's no way Xavi likes me. Not like that."

Suddenly, all I can see is Meritxell. In the dining room. The hall. Every smile.

"So what?" Isa says. "You're still allowed to have a crush."

I drop my pen, and it rolls toward Andy.

"Sorry," I say automatically. It feels like I'm invading a private conversation.

"It's fine." Andy sighs. "Gibs keeps saying I should tell more classmates, or at least the guys on our basketball team. He says no one'll care, but I'm not sure yet.... It's just, y'all three are the only ones who know, and that already feels like a lot."

When neither of them says anything else, I take a breath. "So, you think other boys are cute instead of girls?"

"Yeah." Andy's voice is quiet. "Like, something's always felt off when I went to dances with girls, so I think I've known for a while, but it still feels kind of new to really *know*, you know? That's why I'm not with Madison anymore."

He hands me back my pen. "But since I didn't explain why I broke up with her, she's pretty mad at me."

"Oh, is *that* why she keeps glaring across the dining room?" Isa asks. "I thought she just really hated basketball players."

Andy laughs, but it sputters out fast. "Please don't say anything yet, okay? At least until I figure out how to tell everyone?"

"My lips are sealed." Isa mimes a zipper across their mouth.

They both look at me.

Now might be a good time to share that I think Meritxell is cute the same way Andy likes Xavi. But I still remember how Laurel's friends reacted the first night at dinner.

"I won't say anything, either," I tell him.

That seems to be enough for both of them. I return to my dot diary, while Andy scrolls on his phone and Isa puts their second earbud in. We sit in silence until it's time to head back in. The quiet feels like a soft blanket wrapped around me. Perfect and comfortable.

My alarm goes off for the second time today. I stretch, then twist toward Laurel.

Her bed's empty.

I blink the rest of my grogginess away, wondering if she's in the bathroom. But the light's not on. No sounds come from Sophie-Anne and Madison's room, either.

That's when I see the note on my bedside table.

> El(len),
> Woke up early. Meet you in the dining room!
>
> xo,
>
> (Laur)el

My stomach twists. Laurel left without me.

I get dressed fast and head downstairs to the dining room.

But they're not in our usual spot. Not Laurel. Not Sophie-Anne or Madison. No sign of Meritxell and Xavi, either.

Even Cody's sitting somewhere else, next to Jake and his team. Cody catches my eye, then lifts his shoulders in a small shrug.

"Ellen!" I whirl around, expecting Laurel. But it's Isa who pats the seat next to them.

I grab my breakfast, then head over to my team.

Two teammates, three plates.

"Where's Andy?" I ask.

"Upstairs," says Gibs. "I forgot my meds so he went back for them."

Isa dips their knife into a jar of tomato jam, spreading it onto a piece of baguette. Their plate matches mine: no meat. "Maybe he's hoping to run into *someone* on the way back down."

"Yeah, maybe." Gibs glances from Isa over to me.

"Ellen knows," Isa says. "Andy told her in the garden this morning."

"Oh, cool. Except for the morning part." Gibs spears a piece of jamón with his fork. "I don't know how y'all aren't constant zombies, up that early. I'd sleep in later if Andy would let me."

My eyes follow Gibs's fork to his mouth. "What are the meds for? Or wait, is it rude to ask?"

"It's whatever." He shrugs. "They're supposed to help me concentrate or something."

"That's cool," Isa says. "I mean, at least you've got something that helps."

"I guess." Gibs points his fork at me, twirling it slowly. "Do you take medication for your . . . you know."

"For being autistic?"

"Yeah."

"No. It's just how my brain developed. You can't take medication to change it."

Plus, I like who I am, even if it makes me a little different from everyone else.

Andy enters, then makes his way toward us.

"You should keep these in your backpack." He tosses a small bottle to Gibs. "Hey, Ellen."

"Hi," I say back.

"Dude," Gibs says. "I thought they *were* in my backpack."

As he and Andy debate where his meds were or weren't, I stare at the other table, where I used to sit with Laurel. The boys are talking about the Pla de l'Os mosaic when I notice Mrs. West isn't with Abba and the other adults.

"So, you're still on the second clue, then?" Emmaline's silvery ring flashes as she turns toward Gibs. "We already figured it out. I bet we'll be done with clue three by tonight."

"Cool for you." Gibs shoves a chunk of bread into his mouth.

"I just meant, if your team finishes the clues soon, maybe we can hang out." The entire time Emmaline talks, her eyes stay on Gibs.

"Uh-huh." Gibs flicks a cube of cheese across his plate as the tips of his ears flush pink. "Well, we're not done yet, so..."

Isa and Andy look like they're trying not to laugh, lips quivering. I must've missed the joke.

Before I can ask, Señor L clears his throat and stands. "How's everyone liking the scavenger hunt so far? Having fun, I hope?"

The room gets a little quieter, but no one volunteers to answer.

"Right, well." He waits a beat. "Just a few housekeeping items."

I study his shirt. A cat face smiles out of an avocado halved down the center, right where the pit should be. The text above it reads *Avogato*.

"A reminder that I expect everyone to have gotten through la segunda pista by tomorrow evening."

I'm listening, but I'm also thinking. *Avocado* is English, of course. And *gato* is the Spanish word for "cat." Even though combining them still doesn't make sense to me, I know from my teammates it must be a play on words.

"Then this Saturday, there will be a performance by one of Barcelona's famous casteller troupes, which are also sometimes called human towers." Señor L picks up a piece of paper from the table and waves it. "Here's a sign-up sheet for anyone who'd like to come along. You can also get started on la tercera pista or do some sightseeing if you prefer, so long as there's an adult present."

"Did he say 'human towers'?" Gibs whispers.

Andy keeps his voice low, as well. "Sounds kind of cool."

"I think so, too," says Isa. "Want to go as a team?"

We all nod, and I make a mental note to see if Laurel wants to come.

"The following Friday," Señor L continues, "you'll have the option to watch a movie about Barcelona's unique history."

"That," Isa says, "sounds less cool."

"Next—"

The dining room door swings open before Señor L can go on. Mrs. West enters first, then Madison, Laurel, and Sophie-Anne. Each carries an iced drink, topped with whipped cream.

Isa watches them sit down at my old table. "They seriously went to Starbucks?"

My breakfast swirls in my stomach. Laurel didn't want to wake me up. That made sense. But this feels a whole lot like when she switched seats during the plane trip.

Señor L is also watching the procession. "You're a little late to breakfast, girls."

"It was my fault." Mrs. West flashes him a too-wide smile as she takes a seat beside Abba and the rest of the chaperones. "I invited the girls and just had no idea the line would be so long."

"All right, well." Señor L doesn't seem to know how to respond. He clears his throat and turns back to the rest of us. "Now that everyone's here, I want you all to save space on your schedules for our final Saturday. We'll not only be having dinner at a special, mystery location that evening, but it's also when each team will present a fourth clue."

Every single conversation stops, down to the softest murmur.

"So, hear me out, folks. There are four kids per team—with only one exception." Señor L looks at Emmaline's team of five. "So it makes sense to have each one of y'all present a clue to me and your fellow classmates, en español, of course. Use your tablets and be creative."

The room erupts in excited conversation, Señor L forgotten. I feel a little sick, knowing I'm definitely going to have to present something now that there are four clues.

"He just gave us homework," Gibs mutters. "Well played, Señor L."

Andy shrugs. "It probably won't take long to come up with a clue of our own."

"Plus," Isa says, "we'll finish the second clue today.

We have so much time left, Ellen could pick a place to visit tomorrow, then you the next day"—they point their fork at Gibs—"then Andy and me too, and we'd *still* have almost a week left to solve clue three and decide what we want the fourth to be."

"Okay, okay." Gibs lifts his hands. "I get it."

My gaze drifts. At the other table, Madison and Sophie-Anne have finished their drinks. Laurel's is still half full, probably because she hates coffee.

"That's a really cool idea, actually." Andy's voice pulls me out of my thoughts. "Want to do some sightseeing and save clue three for next week? Once we get done with la segunda pista, I mean."

My thoughts pile up. Another day navigating loud, crowded La Rambla. An unknown location tomorrow.

All without Laurel.

"No," I blurt out.

My teammates look at me.

"No what?" Gibs asks.

I swallow, but the rest of my words stay lodged in my throat. Eyes down, I spot Isa's phone on their lap. I pull mine out and send a message to our group chat.

Ellen

I don't want to go back to La Rambla.

Their phones all chime. Each of my teammates glances down.

Gibs looks up first. "Why not?"

I open my mouth, then close it.

Gibs lifts his phone. "It's cool if you just want to type it."

My teammates wait for me as I choose my words carefully.

Ellen

I want to go back sometime, just need some quiet today. If that's okay?

"I get that." Andy looks up. "Yesterday was pretty hectic."

The swirling in my stomach slows.

"What should we do today instead?" Isa asks.

"Sleep," Gibs says immediately. Then he texts it in all caps to our chat.

Andy ignores him. "There's an FC Barcelona museum that might be cool to visit. FC Barcelona is a club that hosts a lot of sports," he explains. "Basketball, soccer. Probably more."

"I'd skip sleep for that," Gibs says.

"No offense, guys, but I'm not into sports. Are you?"

Isa looks at me and I shake my head. "What if you two ask Mr. Katz to take you and then we can have lunch together before today's field trip? We can even start figuring out what we could do for the fourth clue while you're gone."

"You sure?" Andy asks.

"They just volunteered." Gibs hops up. "Let's go ask Mr. Katz. We can sign up for that human tower thing while we're at it."

"*Isa* volunteered." Andy turns to me. "Are you cool with that plan, too, Ellen?"

I glance at the other table. Laurel smiles at something Sophie-Anne is saying while taking the tiniest sips of her drink.

I turn back to my team. "Yes."

A morning alone with Isa. That's something I can handle.

Chapter Nineteen

Andy hands over the school tablet, then leaves with Gibs and Abba. Isa and I take the stairs back up to the second floor.

"Want to hang out in my room?" Isa asks.

Behind us, footsteps echo in the stairwell. Laurel appears.

"Hey, Elle? Do you have a second to talk?"

I look from Laurel to Isa, who waves me off. "Come over whenever."

I follow Laurel into our room.

"How's your team doing on the clues?" she asks.

"Okay, I think." I'm not sure what she wants to know since we're not supposed to share how we solved them. "We made a mistake at the beginning, but we're figuring things out now."

"That's good." Laurel twists her necklace between two fingers.

"Are you staying here this morning, too?" I ask.

"No." She shakes her head. "I told my team I forgot something up here. I have to go in a sec. It's just"—she sighs—"I thought we'd get to work on the clues today, but Madison wants to go see the Olympic Village."

"Why isn't Mrs. West telling her no?"

"She's doing whatever Madison wants. Because she feels guilty about the divorce or whatever."

"Oh." That could also explain the trip to Starbucks.

"Plus, Madison keeps saying it's not like it'll hurt next year's Spanish grade if we don't solve the clues by the deadline," Laurel says. "I guess it'd just be nice to figure them out together, you know? But I don't want Madison to be mad at me, especially not before cheerleading tryouts in the fall."

I stare at her. "You're quitting gymnastics?"

"I'll do both, if I make the squad."

If Laurel becomes a cheerleader, she'll have even less time for me. Not something I want to think about. I change the subject. "How many clues have you solved so far?"

"None." The word is small. "I tried to translate the first clue on my own, but it didn't make a lot of sense to me, honestly."

I think of how my team works together to translate clues and decide where to visit. It's hard to imagine solving them all by myself.

"Maybe if you share how far you got on your own, they can help you figure out the rest?"

"Maybe." But Laurel keeps fiddling with her necklace. "I know Cody definitely wants to get started. Sophie too, probably."

"Lunch could be a good time to talk about it," I suggest. "When everyone's sitting down and not doing anything else."

"That's a great idea, actually." She smiles, then releases her necklace. "I should go. But thanks, Elle."

"You're welcome."

Laurel turns. I know I should let her go, but my words tumble out before I can stop them. "I miss you."

It's more than that, though. I miss Laurel, of course, but I also miss all the things that make us best friends. Our sleepovers. Special playlists. The stories we make up together.

Laurel twists around. She pulls me into a hug. "I miss you, too. Things would've been so much better if your dad had let you switch teams." Another sigh. "Bye, Elle."

Guilt burrows deep in my stomach. I make my way into Isa's room.

"Hey, everything okay?" they ask.

I shrug, eyes roaming their room. It looks just like Laurel's and mine, except for the orange wall decals.

I set my backpack on the floor, then head to the only window in the room. Instead of the garden, Isa's window overlooks the circular intersection and the pedestrian avenue that leads to the subway station. I look up toward the roof, but no matter how much I twist, the owl remains out of view.

"Yeah, I can't see it, either," Isa says from their bed. "But I bet it's right above us. It'd be so cool to find a way to see it up close."

"So cool," I echo.

Thoughts of Laurel dissolve as Isa drops onto their bed.

"We should ask one of the hotel staff how to get up there."

"Meritxell or Xavi might know," I suggest. "Their family stays here every summer."

Thinking about Meritxell brings a familiar flush to my cheeks, which Isa seems to notice immediately.

"Don't tell me Andy's got even more competition."

I shake my head fast.

Except . . . if I don't have a crush on Xavi that only leaves one other option.

"Wait." Isa sits up. "You like Meritxell?"

I shuffle my feet, not sure where to look.

"You know that's fine, right?"

"Yes."

But as Isa waves me over and I sit at the edge of their bed, shoulders tense, I can't help wondering why it *feels* different to share that I think a girl is cute instead of a boy—especially around Laurel and her friends.

"Just making sure." Isa unlocks the school tablet. I wait for them to ask me more questions, but their eyes stay fixed on the tablet's screen. "I was thinking we could make a collage of the places we already visited before we present our clue. Like a background for our presentation or something. Want to transfer me your pics and then I'll get them all uploaded on here?"

"Sure." I swipe through my photos. Most of them are screenshots of the videos I recorded: our walks to the subway, the inside of La Sagrada Família, two from the La Pedrera courtyard looking up, and one from the roof, looking down.

The longer I swipe, the more my shoulders relax. It was easy to only think about Monday's mistake and yesterday's missed mosaic. These photos are a reminder that my teammates and I have also seen some really cool things.

Same for the videos, but they feel different. I keep them to myself.

"I didn't take many yesterday," I admit. Usually my pics come from screenshots of the videos I take, but I haven't looked at my videos of La Rambla yet.

"That's okay. I've got plenty, and I'm sure I can get more from Andy and Gibs. Except, this tablet isn't connecting to the hotel Wi-Fi for some reason." Isa twists in bed, then pulls their phone cord out of the wall and connects it to the tablet. "It could be worse," Isa continues. "Back home, my dad still has this super old laptop that uses a USB-A cord. Talk about stuff that belongs in a museum."

"Do you know a lot about computers?" I ask.

"I know a little about a lot of things." Isa starts the photo transfer, and the tablet fills with a colorful array of images. "I like knowing how stuff works. I really want to make something completely new someday. Something that no one's ever done before."

"Like what would you make?"

"Not sure yet." Isa's eyes stay on the tablet. "But I listen to a ton of podcasts about how people make things, like woodworkers and architects, artists and computer programmers. I have my favorite shows on, like, a constant stream, just in case something gives me an idea."

So that's what Isa's always listening to.

They turn back to the tablet, humming a little. My mind wanders as they click through newly uploaded photos, first to what Isa learned about Meritxell and me, then to Andy and Xavi.

I look back at Isa. "I have a question."

The photos stop flickering as Isa's finger hovers above the screen. "I have an answer. Possibly."

"Do you like boys or girls?" I ask. "Or other nonbinary people?"

"You mean like what types of people do I get crushes on?"

"Yes." My face heats up as doubt forms in my stomach. "Is that a rude question?"

"Some people might think so, but it's not to me," Isa says. "And I like everyone."

"Everyone?" I study Isa, wondering if they're joking. But the corners of their mouth don't turn up. Their lips don't quiver like they're trying to hold back laughter.

"Well, not *everyone* everyone. I just mean I don't care if you're a boy or a girl or something else. If I like you, I like you. Does that make sense?"

It's new for me, just like having the extra pronouns list in my dot diary. "I think so."

"Cool." Isa finishes flipping through pictures we took at La Sagrada Família and moves on to La Pedrera. "Now, if I ask you a question, too, will you also tell me if it's rude?"

"Yes."

"Do you only like girls?"

"Um"—I completely forget to tell Isa if their question's rude or not—"all I know is I have never thought a boy is cute."

"That's cool," Isa says again. Now their cheeks look a little rosy, too.

As they move on to La Rambla photos, I think through what I just shared. I sort of said I liked girls, just in a more rambling way.

Kind of?

Isa sits back. "This part might be tricky if we don't have the boys' photos. Let's save the actual collage for later and make the guys do some of that work."

"Okay."

"I have another idea.... We could invite Meritxell and Xavi to have lunch at that boquería by the subway after we get back from La Rambla tomorrow. You know, since Andy's too shy to do it himself?"

"Right...."

"But," Isa rushes on, "if that'd make you uncomfortable, like with Meritxell there and everything, we can just watch a movie. I've got lots on my iPad, if you're okay with Disney."

I take a moment to think. The only reason I'm in Isa's room today instead of overwhelmed on La Rambla is because my teammates changed their schedule for me.

"I want to just watch a movie," I tell Isa, "but I also want to do something nice for Andy."

We head to the ground floor. But the closer I get to Meritxell's hotel room, the more my insides knot and twist.

We pause in front of the door, and I turn to Isa. "Can you talk to them? Is that okay?"

"Sure."

They knock and the door swings open, revealing Meritxell and a glimpse of what looks like a multi-room apartment.

"¿Qui és?" Xavi's voice drifts to us, and Meritxell replies back with fast, unfamiliar words.

Who is it? in Spanish is "¿Quién es?" So maybe what Xavi just said is in Catalan. I want to ask, but my throat goes dry.

"Hi!" Isa waves. "We were wondering if you and Xavi want to have lunch with us tomorrow."

"You are so nice," Meritxell says, and my chest fills with butterflies. "But I'm sorry. Tomorrow, Xavi and I have plans already."

"Oh, okay." Isa takes a step back, and I copy them. "No worries."

The fluttering fades. Disappointment arrives in its place.

"What about Saturday?" I blurt out.

For a moment, Isa just looks at me. Then their brows rise. "Oh yeah! Are you and Xavi maybe free then? We're going to see castellers with our teacher after breakfast."

"Ah, vale," Meritxell says. "Yes, we are free then."

"Even Xavi?" I make myself ask.

"Even Xavi what?" Xavi calls. It's the first thing I've heard him say in English.

Meritxell ignores him. "Yes, Xavi too. I'll make him come since he is too lazy to get out of bed now and decide for himself. We will see you Saturday."

As soon as she closes her door, Isa pumps their fists, reminding me of Gibs.

"Mission accomplished." They grin. "Plus, you talked to Meritxell!"

I duck my head. "It was for Andy."

"Yeah, but still." We head back upstairs. "You're braver than you think, Ellen."

This time, when the warm, fluttery feeling returns, I'm not even thinking about Meritxell.

Chapter Twenty

Day 6

The following afternoon, my classmates and I return to the hotel after our field trip to the Picasso Museum. It was a long day, but it felt good going back to La Rambla this morning. My headphones kept the noise manageable, and it helped knowing all the side streets led back to La Rambla. Even when we took a wrong turn, all we had to do was switch directions. Pla de l'Os wasn't hard to find, and we got back to the hotel in plenty of time for lunch before we headed to the museum.

Andy pauses on the girls-plus-Isa floor landing. "Want to talk to Señor L before the siesta to finish our second clue?"

Gibs and Isa nod.

"Okay," Andy says. "Who wants to do this one?"

I raise my hand like I'm answering a question in class.

"You sure?" Andy asks.

"Yes." I practiced last night, until I had every word memorized.

We follow Andy up to the boys' floor. He catches up with Señor L midway down the hall.

"¡Buenas tardes!" Señor L says.

"Is now an okay time to recite our clue?" Isa asks.

"Pregúntame en español, por favor."

"Oh." Isa clears their throat, then repeats their question in Spanish for Señor L, who nods to let us know he's ready.

"Ellen's got this one," Isa says.

I take a calming breath, then reach into my pocket for the clue sheet.

A door opens down the hall. Jake appears with his roommate, Daniel.

Señor L looks past me. "Hello, boys."

Before they can respond, Emmaline and Clara appear by the stairs. Another door opens, revealing their final teammate, Peter. They make their way over to us as a group.

"Come to show me how you solved the third clue?" Señor L smiles.

"Yep." Emmaline glances our way, fluttering her fingers at Gibs in a quick wave.

"Qué bien." Señor L turns to our team. "And if I remember correctly, y'all're on la segunda pista, ¿verdad?"

We nod.

"Let's have your team go first then. Once you're done, I'll listen to the next team so no one overhears anything they shouldn't." He looks over at me. "You're up, Miss Katz."

Suddenly, my audience has doubled. My thoughts scatter. I try to swallow, but my mouth's gone dry. This isn't what I imagined when I practiced last night.

"Ellen?" Señor L prompts.

But I can't. My words aren't just stuck, they've taken off faster than Gibs when he spots something interesting.

Gibs steps forward. "Actually, I'll do this one."

He holds out a hand, and I let him take my clue sheet. Gibs recites the clue in Spanish, then shares our translation. As he describes the street performers we saw, the colorful tiles of Pla de l'Os, and the Port Vell tapas, Andy and Isa show Señor L photos they took on their phones.

"Muy bien. You're making good progress." Señor L hands us each a new clue sheet. "Buena suerte on this next one!"

My chest clenches as I follow my team down the hallway. We stop in front of room 3C.

"You okay, Ellen?" Andy whispers as Gibs digs out a key.

I round my shoulders. "Sorry," I whisper back.

"No big deal," Gibs says. "We solved the clue. You can do the next one, no problem."

Isa nods. None of them seem mad.

"Okay." My shoulders relax. "I'll do the next one."

Isa and I say goodbye to the boys and head downstairs.

"Two down, one to go." Isa waves as they disappear into their room. "See you at dinner."

My room is empty when I enter. A muffled murmur of voices reaches me from one room over. Maybe Laurel and her team are working on the clues. She seemed so hopeful last night after dinner, telling me how her team helped her translate more of the first clue at lunch, just like I suggested. Then this morning, she was practically bouncing at the thought of finally starting the scavenger hunt.

Laurel's making progress on the clues, and my team has been there for me when I've needed them. Everything's working out, even if it's not exactly the way I expected. For both of us.

I settle on my bed with my dot diary, planning to update it with tomorrow's excursion. The postcards I bought on my first visit to La Rambla lie between the front cover and first page.

The owl card seems to beckon to me. I pick it up, then flip it around. Isa's list of puns had a lot of animal references, mostly words that sounded like others. *Gopher* for *go for*, *toucan* for *two can*, *cheetah* for *cheater*, and *lion* for *lying*.

Nothing about owls, though.

I think about words that sound like *owl*, then jot down a line on the back of the card and read it to myself. It's simple, but perfect because I created it all on my own.

A happy feeling bubbles inside me. I flap my hands, and the feeling spreads from my chest into my arms and legs. When I rock, it's usually because there's too much going on and rocking helps calm me. Flapping is different because it lets me feel more. Every little ounce of joy, amplified.

By the time I stop, my body is alive with energy. It's almost time for dinner, then a call with Mom before Shabbat. I twist in bed, wedging my owl postcard between the frame and wall near my pillow. Now I can look at it whenever I want.

I head to the dining room. Laurel's already sitting with her team. She looks up when I enter. I wave at her, then make my way to my teammates.

Two clues down, like Isa said. Deadline met. I've got this.

After dinner, I retrace my steps to the boys' floor.

"Hi, metukah." Abba lets me in, and I settle onto his bed. A brown paper bag near one pillow crinkles as he sits down next to me. "Hard to believe it's been a whole week already. Are you having a good time?"

"Yes."

"Glad to hear it." Abba leans back. "Ready to call home?"

"Very ready." Laurel isn't the only one I've missed on this trip.

Abba taps into Mom's contact page on his iPad, then clicks the video chat button.

"Good afternoon, my loves!" Mom waves at us. "How was your week?"

Abba sits back on his pillow, letting me answer.

"It's been good."

"Have you solved any more scavenger hunt clues?"

"Yes." I tell Mom about La Rambla, about how loud and bright and crowded it was. "We had to go back today to finish the clue, but my team didn't seem to mind."

"It sounds like you're on a very good team," Mom

says. "When one person needs a little extra support, the others help them out."

I nod. That's exactly how it feels. "Have you finished your cross-stitch project yet?"

"Not exactly." Mom chuckles. "But . . . actually, just a minute."

She disappears, then returns a second later. "Ta-da!"

She holds up something small, green, and spiky. "His name is David."

Abba leans closer to the screen. "Is that—"

"A cactus?" I squint at it.

Mom nods, her hair swishing around her chin.

"Miriam," Abba says. "I don't mean to be negative, but do you remember what happened the last time you got a plant?"

"Vincent the fern," I murmur, remembering the little plant that once sat on our kitchen windowsill. "May his memory be a blessing."

"A cactus is different, Natan," Mom says. "You don't have to water them every day. Plus, I needed something to keep me company while the two of you are off traveling the world."

"Fine, fine," Abba says before I can tell Mom that visiting one country doesn't make us world travelers. He turns to me. "Are you okay with a hug?"

I nod. He wraps his arms around me, then looks back at the screen.

"We miss you, too, ahuvati, and hope David keeps you company. Right, Elle-bell?"

"Yes." My hair bounces as I nod again. "We'll be home soon."

"I know. And you can meet David when you get back," Mom says. "Because he definitely won't be dead."

"Be'ezrat Hashem." Abba grins.

David the cactus will live, Abba is saying, but only with divine intervention.

"It's getting close to sundown here," Abba says. "During siesta time today, I visited a local market. Couldn't find any actual Shabbat candles, unfortunately, but look."

He reaches for the paper bag and pulls out a small box.

Mom laughs. "Seriously, Natan?"

I study the box's contents. "They look like they're for a birthday cake."

"It was either these or one of the big candles with a Catholic saint sticker." Abba gets up and digs through his suitcase. He returns with his kippah and some silver hair clips, then points to something on his desk.

"Unfortunately, I also couldn't find a candleholder. But hopefully this will work."

I immediately recognize the rectangular pale-blue

bar of soap. We have the same kind in our bathroom, although Laurel, Sophie-Anne, and Madison seem to prefer the bodywash they brought from home.

Abba's carved two little grooves in it. A makeshift candleholder.

"Would you like to do the honors and welcome the Shabbat Queen tonight, Elle-bell?"

"Yes."

Abba passes me two candles. I get up and fit them into the soap holder as Abba lights a match. He passes it to me. Once both tiny flames sway in front of me, I shield my eyes with both hands.

"Baruch atah Adonai, Eloheinu, melekh ha'olam..." I recite the blessing we say each Friday night. If Spanish were this easy for me, I wouldn't have needed Gibs to recite the second clue earlier.

"Yafeh me'od," Abba says when I finish.

Mom nods, too, letting me know I did a good job. "How about a song to celebrate Shabbat? Let's do 'Lekha Dodi.'"

I rejoin Abba on the bed. Mom takes a breath, then hums a tune so Abba and I can follow along. There are many ways to sing Shabbat songs. Some melodies are traditional, slow and haunting. Some sound modern.

Tonight, Mom's voice is light and upbeat as she starts to sing.

By the end of the first verse, Abba joins in, then I do. He sways as he sings, and both little candle flames dance a couple of feet away on his desk. Our voices are our own, Mom's high, Abba's deep and low. Mine falls somewhere in between. The song feels like a big, warm hug with me wrapped in the middle between Abba and Mom.

Even though we're half a world away from Mom, Shabbat brings us all home.

Chapter Twenty-One
Day 7

Saturday is the first day I blink the sleep out of my eyes, reach for my phone, and see that it's not 4:00 a.m.

I completely missed our garden meetup.

I click through to a pair of notifications in the group chat. Around 4:30 a.m., Andy and Isa both said they missed me. I type back a quick response.

Ellen
Sorry I didn't come down this morning. I didn't wake up until now.

A message pings back.

Isa (they/them)
It's cool. Glad you got some sleep!

Isa (they/them)

What are the odds your dad's awake? I kinda want
to check out a cafe down the street

Ellen

50/50. Meet you in five minutes?

Isa (they/them)

K!

Isa (they/them)

Andy and Gibs can come too if they're awake, hint
hiiiiint

I get dressed fast and grab my backpack, then make
my way over to Laurel's bed.

"Good morning."

She groans and squeezes her eyes shut tighter.

"My team is going to a café before breakfast," I try
again. "Want to come?"

"Too tired," Laurel mumbles.

"There'll probably be lots of interesting people to
see . . . lots of stories we can come up with."

Nothing.

I swallow down my disappointment, trying not to
feel hurt that Laurel would rather sleep than hang out
with me.

"Do you at least have the main key still?" Abba has

one, and so do my other teammates, but Laurel's kept our only copy in her purse since the day we got here.

When Laurel still doesn't respond, I head out, letting the door click shut loudly behind me.

Isa appears a moment later. "Morning!"

"Morning." I chew on the inside of my cheek.

If they notice my tension, they don't mention it as we head upstairs. The boys still haven't responded by the time we get Abba, so we leave the hotel without them.

Even this early in the morning, people are out. But no one seems like they're rushing today. The sidewalks feel calmer and quieter. I definitely don't need my headphones.

Isa leads us down the street. "I saw a café on the walk to the subway on our first day. Everyone online says to try the donuts. They make them fresh and don't put in the custard until you've ordered."

"That sounds really good," I tell them.

Inside the café, we wait in a short line. As Abba orders coffee, I study a row of open-faced sandwiches in a glass display. Each has the same thin-sliced meat the hotel serves. Jamón serrano.

"What does that taste like?" I ask Isa, suddenly curious.

"What? The sandwiches?"

I nod. "Meritxell said it's a specialty, but I can't try it since it's not kosher."

"Oh. No clue." Isa shrugs. "I've never tried it, either."

"Really?"

"Well, yeah. I'm vegetarian. But I bet Andy or Gibs could tell you."

"Meet you two outside," Abba calls as the server returns with his coffee.

Isa leans toward the display counter and asks the server a question in Spanish. They bounce on the balls of their feet at the response, then turn to me. "They make natillas here!"

"Natillas?" I'm still stuck on the fact that Isa's a vegetarian. They've probably been eating the exact same things as Abba and me this whole trip.

Isa breaks out in a big grin. "You'll see. What custard do you want in your donut: vanilla or chocolate?"

"Hmm...vanilla."

"Cool. I'll get some for the boys, too. Oversleeping beggars can't be choosers, so I'll get one chocolate and one vanilla, then they can figure out who gets which."

I pass Isa some money for my donut, stealing a glance at them while they pay the cashier. "You know more Spanish than the rest of us."

Isa pockets the change. "Why do you think that?"

"It's just, you seem to understand what people say

better than anyone, except maybe Señor L. Plus your accent sounds perfect."

The server hands a box of donuts to Isa along with a container in a paper bag. We head toward the exit.

"I'm not fluent in Spanish," Isa says. "Not even close. But I can say some basic stuff. None of my grandparents taught my parents Spanish because they didn't want them to have an accent. I'm definitely still learning."

I think this through as we walk back toward the hotel with Abba. Everyone always seems impressed when they find out I know Hebrew. And I've never heard anyone say anything mean to Abba, even though he has an accent. "Isn't being bilingual a good thing?"

"It's different for some people," Isa says. "White people only seem to think it's cool if other white people can speak multiple languages. No offense."

"None taken," Abba says. "It is certainly a double standard."

"Yeah. So it gets annoying when people just assume I know Spanish because of my last name or how I look. I know Gibs was just being Gibs, but that's why I called him out when he wanted me to translate the first clue on my own."

Abba unlocks the hotel's front door, then holds it open for us.

"That makes sense," I say. "Although it'd be cool if

we could all just automatically speak languages from the places our families are originally from."

"For real." Isa checks their phone. "The boys are awake. They'll meet us in the dining room."

"As will I," Abba says. "After I make a quick detour to get my iPad. Inspiration never sleeps, regardless of the time zone."

Isa and I claim our usual seats in the dining room. Although it's earlier than when our group meets for breakfast, other hotel guests eat, read newspapers, and sip coffee.

"I bet you they get here early to avoid us," Isa says. "We can be pretty loud."

"No bet," I tell Isa because I'm positive they're correct.

Andy and Gibs arrive, then grab breakfast and sit down with us. Abba picks a spot on his own when he returns with his iPad a few minutes later.

"We got you both donuts, but you'll have to decide who gets which flavor," Isa tells Andy and Gibs.

I like the way Isa says "we," like the two of us are a team.

"I'm fine with either," Andy says.

"Sweet." Gibs grabs the chocolate donut and digs in immediately.

I take a small bite of my donut, eyes on Isa as they pull the container out of the paper bag.

"What is that?" Gibs's words are a little garbled, his mouth full of custard.

"Natillas," Isa says. "It looks a little different from what my grandma makes, but I had to try it." They peel back the container lid, revealing a yellow custard sprinkled with cinnamon. "We can share if anyone else wants some."

We each grab a spoon, and Isa takes the first bite. "I think I like the creamier version my grandma makes more, but this is still good."

I let the sweet flavor linger on my tongue as Isa turns to Andy.

"Ellen and I have a surprise for you."

"Yeah?"

Andy chews a piece of baguette and waits for us to go on as our classmates start to file in. The moment the other hotel guests spot them, they stand to leave, making me glad I didn't take Isa's bet.

"We invited Meritxell and Xavi to come with us today." Isa's voice pulls me back to my own table.

"You did?" Andy's eyes widen. "When?"

"Thursday," I say. "While you and Gibs were visiting the sports museum."

"Yeah." Isa scans the dining room. "Hopefully they didn't forget about it...."

Andy nudges a piece of meat with his fork without a word.

"We didn't say anything about you specifically," I offer. "Just that we wanted to hang out."

"Oh, okay." Finally, Andy smiles. "That sounds fun. I mean, if they remember to come."

"Yep." Isa dips their spoon into the natillas container.

Señor L enters and heads up toward the chaperone part of our table.

"Buenos días," he calls.

A couple of students, including Andy, say good morning back to him, although most stay focused on their own conversations.

"Anyway, thanks." Andy looks over at Isa and me. "For asking Xavi, I mean. It'll be cool to get to hang out."

Once everyone's back in their seats, Señor L speaks again. "I hope each of you is having fun with the scavenger hunt so far. Y'all've made great progress, for the most part."

I glance over at Laurel, who's staring at her plate like she's going to be quizzed on it later. I wonder if her team received their second clue yet.

"Those who signed up for the casteller performance," he continues, "please meet me down on the ground floor after breakfast."

The dining room doors don't open again until we're done with breakfast, almost ready to head out.

Meritxell's long, flowery skirt ripples as she makes

her way over to us. "We're late," she says. "Xavi didn't wake up on time, again."

Xavi smirks, and Andy looks down at his hands. I think I know how he feels.

"I sleep through my alarm literally every day," Gibs says, like it's something he's proud of.

Around us, kids start to stand.

"You didn't get to eat," Andy says, eyes darting from Xavi to the buffet.

"It's okay." Meritxell dismisses him with a wave. "There are many cafés in the city, with better food. We will eat soon."

I look over at Abba. "Are you coming?"

It takes him a moment to look up from his iPad. "I'm actually going to stay here today and get some work done. If you need anything, your teacher and the other chaperones will be there the entire time, though. Sound good?"

A twinge of discomfort. I shake it off and change the subject.

"The community room is more comfortable if you don't need a table."

"A great idea, metukah." Abba stands and rolls out his neck. "See you when you get back."

We follow the rest of our classmates downstairs. It looks like everyone's signed up to see the castellers, even Laurel's team.

The moment we're outside, Laurel grabs my hand and pulls me toward her team near the back of the group. The unexpected touch sends needle pricks up my arm. I suck in a sharp breath but don't pull away.

"Madison wants to avoid Andy," she whispers.

"Oh, okay." I exhale, and the feeling fades.

Isa looks back at us but doesn't wave for me to come join them.

We take the subway and transfer to a line that goes toward Plaça de Catalunya, where Señor L says we'll need to transfer again. I stand with Laurel's team, holding a pole to help keep my balance as the train speeds through an underground tunnel. Meritxell and Xavi stand between our group and Andy, Gibs, and Isa. We squeeze closer to each other as more riders board at the next stop.

"Does anyone else think those human towers sound super boring?"

I glance over at Madison.

"Kind of, I guess?" Sophie-Anne shrugs as Laurel nods.

Cody silently watches the exchange.

"I actually have an idea," Madison whispers. "I overheard Sully talking about the second clue. It's totally at La Rambla, so let's go there instead."

"La Rambla has great shopping."

We all look over at Meritxell.

"Y comida," adds Xavi. He must be hungry.

Finally, Cody speaks up. "We don't even have the second clue sheet yet."

"Who even cares?" Madison shoots back. "We can just take pics of everything, then figure out the first clue tomorrow. We'll be working on clue three by Monday, just like everyone else."

I grip the pole tighter. They haven't even figured out la primera pista yet? What were they doing yesterday, then?

"If you go to La Rambla, Xavi and I will come with you," Meritxell says.

My fingers start to ache.

"I want to see the castellers," Cody says.

"Then go." Madison flutters her fingers at him.

The train slows at the Catalunya stop. We all get out.

"Mom!" Madison yells. "Change of plans."

I hesitate, glancing at Meritxell and Xavi. "But don't you want to hang out and see the castellers with my team?"

Meritxell says something to Xavi, probably in Catalan.

"Xavi and I have seen the castellers many times. They're boring to us."

My stomach ties itself into knots. It's suddenly hard to remember what I admired about Meritxell's honesty.

"Will you come, too?" Meritxell asks me.

"Hey, y'all," Señor L calls. "What's the holdup?"

Mrs. West turns to us. "Just a moment, girls. I'll talk to him."

I watch the two of them carefully. Señor L crosses his arms, then relaxes them the more Mrs. West talks. He lifts one hand and seems to be counting students. Finally, he clears his throat.

"Slight change of plans." His voice rises over the noise of an approaching train. "Mrs. West will be taking a group to La Rambla. If anyone wants to go there instead, speak now or forever hold your peace."

My teammates look back at me, but a hand slips into mine before I can say anything.

"Stay with us, Elle?" Laurel asks.

"But . . ." My tongue feels thick. "I've already been to La Rambla."

Twice.

"So have we," Laurel says. "Come with us. *Please?* I really want to hang out with you today."

I don't know how I can feel happy and upset all at once.

"Do you want to go to La Rambla today instead?" I ask my team.

I already know the answer before they shake their heads.

"Is it okay if I go?" The words come out quieter this time, more uncertain.

"It's your choice." Andy looks away, and guilt flares in my chest.

I raise my hand, not sure I can speak loud enough for Señor L to hear.

"All right," he says when he spots me. "Everyone else ready?"

Laurel squeals just like Sophie-Anne, and I cover my ears automatically.

"Sorry!" Laurel's hand flies to her mouth. "I'm just excited."

As the rest of my classmates disappear down a tunnel to transfer lines, Laurel leads me in the opposite direction, toward the stairs that will lead us out of the station.

Your choice. Andy's voice rings in my ears as I walk away from my team and my schedule.

Chapter Twenty-Two

People. Everywhere.

Flooding out of the station.

Taking pictures.

Horns honking.

Pigeons squawk, squawk, squawking.

Performers twirl in shiny costumes.

Meritxell points toward the familiar MERCAT: ST JOSEP sign. "The boquería has good food and drinks."

People pack the boquería's entrance, standing shoulder to shoulder, brushing past each other.

My hands shake as we cross the street.

"Hoo-wee." Mrs. West fans herself in front of a restaurant at the edge of the market. "I think I'll stay here and order a cold drink. Y'all have fun and come get me when you're done."

Panic grips my ribs and squeezes. She's really going to leave us alone in this?

I slip my backpack off one shoulder and reach for my headphones. At least there's one thing I can be in control of here.

"This way." Meritxell seems to smile directly at me as she waves us forward.

My fingers brush against my headphone case, hesitating. Meritxell and Xavi quickly disappear into the crowd. The other girls form a single-file line and follow them, phones out and snapping photos. I slide my bag back into place.

Shopkeepers call out to potential customers:

¡Marisco!

¡Dulces y chocolate!

¡Jamón Ibérico!

Sweat beads along my back. The air feels thick.

I'm glad I just have to follow, because I can't decide where to look. Noises warp into colors that pulse behind my eyes. Clicks, clacks, thuds, and slams come at me from every direction in oranges, browns, yellows, reds.

My phone pings against my leg, a vibration that stings. I silence it.

By the time we come to a stop, my whole body aches.

I reach into my backpack a second time, slipping on my headphones. The noise level drops. Immediate relief.

Meritxell pauses in front of rows of colorful drinks: a rainbow of juice cups. She and Xavi pay for a pair, then wait for us to choose.

"I tried these when my family was here last year," Madison says. "Strawberry's the best."

Laurel reaches for one of the pink drinks.

Sophie-Anne reaches in the same direction, but hesitates, glancing at Madison and then back to the cups before choosing orange.

Laurel turns to me. "Which one do you want, Elle?"

I study the cups, trying to guess what flavor lines up with each color.

A hand waves in my face. "Helloooo?"

I step back fast, blinking Madison into focus.

"It's kind of rude to have those on when we're hanging out." She points to her ears, then mine. "Can you even hear anything we're saying?"

Isa told me no one would mind if I wore my headphones earlier this week. Now Madison's saying the opposite.

"I can hear you."

"O-kay." One simple word, but it transports me back to our first night in Barcelona. My stomach twists. I look up and spot Meritxell, watching us.

I slide my headphones off. Slip them back into my bag.

"Did you want to get a drink, Elle?" Laurel asks again.

I shake my head.

The other girls pay and we move on, stopping at a kiosk so Madison can buy chocolates shaped like a bouquet of roses.

Laurel buys a small jar of saffron for her mom at a spice stand, then Sophie-Anne orders a paper cup filled with jamón jerky slices. She offers it around. Madison and Laurel take some. Xavi takes a lot. I shake my head when she stops in front of me.

"Oh, sorry! I forgot you don't eat certain foods."

"That's right." The list fills my thoughts, each word parading behind my eyes. "No pork, no shrimp—"

"Your dad does."

All of us turn to Madison.

"What?" I swallow hard, trying to keep the rest of my list down.

"He ordered shrimp paella when we went out for dinner. Or maybe it was prawn."

"No he didn't." I take a shallow breath. "He wouldn't."

She shrugs. "Except I saw him."

"Okay, y'all. It doesn't really matter, right?" I turn, expecting Laurel, but it's Sophie-Anne who spoke. Nearby, Laurel sips her drink, completely silent.

Needles again. This time they don't just prickle, they burrow deep into my skin.

We stop in front of a tapas stand for Xavi. I had such good plans for today. I was going to talk to Meritxell, ask her about the Catalan language. Andy and Xavi were supposed to hang out.

Instead, I'm somewhere that's too-bright, too-loud, too-many-smells. My throat's too tight to talk to anyone, and Xavi ducks in and out of aisles, barely spending time with us.

It doesn't really matter. That's what Sophie-Anne said. But all of this matters to me, from the last-minute decision to change plans to Madison's claim about Abba.

The sounds start building up in my head again. Soon, my ears pound in time with my pulse. Conversations buzz around me, but the words mean nothing.

"Are you okay?"

It takes me a second to focus on Laurel, but I can't answer. Can hardly understand her.

She turns to Sophie-Anne and Madison, who've stopped to take photos of dried peppers hung up like decorations. They look over at me. Meritxell and Xavi stand nearby, watching, watching, watching.

Laurel takes my hand. It stings, but I don't have the energy to pull away.

I keep my eyes on my feet, letting her guide me back to Mrs. West. We all leave the boquería together.

My pulse still pounds. I narrow my eyes to keep the light and colors out.

But sneakers still squeak on the pavement.

The hot air clogs my lungs.

Coins clink in performers' cups.

So many different languages, spoken all at once.

Then, quiet, except for some indistinct, whispered words from Sophie-Anne.

Or maybe it's Madison.

Air-conditioning.

Little by little, the world comes back to me.

I open my eyes a bit more. Dresses and skirts hang from every wall. Peasant-style blouses at the center of the shop, sandals lined up on a rack near the back. Our group is alone here, except for the store clerk.

"Is this better, Elle?"

Words make sense again. Relief floods through me. "Yes."

"Okay, good." Laurel lets out a long breath, shoulders lowering. "Want to look at some dresses while we're here?"

What I really want to do is rock, but not in front of Mrs. West. Not in front of Sophie-Anne, or Madison, and especially not Meritxell and Xavi. When I don't answer, Laurel waves me toward a row of dresses.

As she holds a purple dress up in front of a mirror, I touch a blue skirt's gauzy, soft fabric.

"That's super pretty, Ellen." Sophie-Anne stops beside me.

"Yeah," Laurel agrees. "That color would look great on you."

"Are you thinking of buying it?" Sophie-Anne asks.

"No." I frown. "Skirts are uncomfortable."

I know this is an opinion, not a fact. Something Dr. Talia says I should try to distinguish when I'm having a conversation. Just because I don't like something doesn't make it bad.

"Oh." Sophie-Anne blinks. "Okay."

Before I can apologize—or decide if I even need to—Sophie-Anne's already gone, heading over to Madison.

Nearby, Meritxell and Xavi talk in low tones.

"I think we will go now," Meritxell says. "We don't want to buy dresses. Especially Xavi."

Xavi rolls his eyes, and I can't help feeling he would've had a much better time with Andy.

"But thank you for inviting us." Meritxell looks at me when she says this. My chest doesn't flutter. All I feel is heavy. Tired.

The other girls wave goodbye, then return to their shopping.

Soon, Laurel drapes two dresses over one arm.

Sophie-Anne and Madison head toward a changing area with their own selections. Laurel hesitates.

"I'm sorry today hasn't been fun for you." She keeps her voice down, like she's sharing a secret. "Want to have a sleepover tonight, like we used to?"

"But we're already in the same hotel room."

"Well, yeah," Laurel says. "But we can make it feel like a sleepover. Like, we can stream a movie or listen to music. Whatever you want."

The knots in my stomach loosen. "All right."

"I'm going to try these on." Laurel holds up the dresses. "Come with me?"

A Saturday night sleepover, just like we used to do. I take a deep breath, letting the cool air settle in my chest. The quiet in the shop soothes me even more. I follow Laurel back to the dressing area, feeling lighter already.

Chapter Twenty-Three

Later that evening, I help Laurel move her bed up against mine.

She grabs her iPad and props it up against a pillow. "What do you want to watch?"

"I don't know," I admit. I actually want to watch *The Emperor's New Groove*, but Laurel stopped wanting to watch Disney movies a couple of years ago.

"Sophie told me about a cheerleading docuseries on YouTube." Laurel taps into the app. "If you don't care what we watch, maybe we could start that?"

Not knowing and not caring are two different things, but Laurel's already clicked on the first episode.

We watch interviews with high school freshmen and sophomores hoping to make their school's junior varsity team. It's not the most interesting thing ever, but

Laurel's eyes stay fixed on the screen as the cheerleading hopefuls move on to tryouts in the second episode.

"This is nice," I say as the video switches from interviews to a montage of tumbling passes. "I feel so much calmer now."

"Awesome." Laurel throws a smile my way. "It's definitely quieter than at La Rambla."

Laurel's gaze returns to the screen, and I pull out my phone to a mountain of notifications. I forgot I'd silenced it earlier.

Andy (he/him)
Hope you had fun today, Ellen!
Isa (they/them)
The castellers were amazing.
Gibs (a dude)
Still super bummed they didn't take volunteers.
I would've made a great addition to the human tower
Isa (they/them)
You would've died
Isa (they/them)
Here's what it looked like, Ellen!

I click the photo they sent. Over a dozen people stand on the ground in a circle. They all wear white pants with black sashes around their waists. Each person holds the ankles of another performer, standing on their shoulders. The castell narrows the higher I look, until there's just one person at the top.

Andy (he/him)
We also talked about where we want to go after we figure out the third clue.
Gibs (a dude)
Park with the 🦎!
Isa (they/them)
But only if that's okay with you, Ellen

There are other texts, but I reply to Isa's first.

Ellen
That's fine with me. Also, I looked it up and El Drac means "The Dragon" in Catalan.

Isa responds immediately.

Isa (they/them)
Might need to rethink some things, Gibs!
Gibs (a dude)
DRAGONS ARE JUST BIG LIZARDS

I laugh and Laurel looks over at me.

"What?"

"Nothing," I say. "My team's just being silly."

"Ah." She glances back at her iPad. The squad's been chosen now, and they're gearing up for their first event. "So, you're having fun with them and getting through the clues okay?"

Two questions in one, but both have the same answer, which makes things simpler. "Yes."

I glance at my phone again and notice Andy's added pronouns next to his name. Same for Gibs, in his own way. I tap into my profile and update my display name.

"That's nice." Laurel sighs.

I'm about to ask her what's wrong when my phone buzzes again.

Isa (they/them)
Anyway…are we hanging out in the garden
tonight?
Gibs (a dude)
lolnope zzz
Andy (he/him)
I'm down. Same time as usual?

I look from my phone to Laurel, then back again.

Ellen (she/her/hers)

I can't tonight. I'm hanging out with Laurel.

Isa (they/them)

That's cool. There's always tomorrow!

Gibs (a dude)

"Okay, I think I need a break." Laurel pauses the video after the homecoming football game episode. "How do you feel about makeovers?"

"Like in general?"

"I mean for us." She makes the mattress bounce. "Tonight."

Laurel should know I'm not interested. But something seemed wrong earlier, so I offer a compromise.

"Not for me. But we can do your hair and makeup together."

"That works!" Laurel hops up. "I want to see what looks best with my new dress."

I follow her to the bathroom.

"Plus, you're so honest, you can give me your opinion," she says. "That'll help a ton."

A flash of guilt. I definitely wasn't honest about asking Abba to switch teams. After today with Meritxell, I'm not even sure being honest all the time is a good thing.

Laurel flips on the bathroom light and empties her

makeup bag. "I usually like pastels, but I don't think they'll look right with my new dress. Actually, hold that thought. I'll go put it on!"

As she scampers back into the bedroom, I scan the counter. Blush. Eye shadow. Mascara. Four different colors of lip gloss. I organize them alphabetically on the counter: cheeks, eyelids, lashes, mouth.

Laurel opens the door wider and twirls. "What do you think?"

"It's very purple."

"So purple. I adore it." She grins.

"Is someone in there?" Sophie-Anne calls from the other room.

"Yes, but you can come in!" Laurel calls back.

The door swings open.

"Oh my actual gosh, Laurel," Sophie-Anne says, "that dress!"

Laurel looks down, then lifts the skirt. "You think?"

"So. Cute."

It's like they're speaking a different language in half sentences.

Madison appears in the doorway. "FYI: perfect shade."

Laurel beams. "We were just going to see what makeup and hair works best with it."

"I want to help!" Sophie-Anne claps, and I take a step

back, bumping into the towel hanger. "We should all try on our dresses and give ourselves makeovers."

"We totally should," Laurel says.

"Be right back!" Sophie-Anne takes off with Madison.

"That's okay, right, Elle?" Laurel looks at me.

The smile hasn't left her face since the other girls arrived.

I make myself nod.

So much for being honest.

Half an hour later, all three girls are in full makeup. They've straightened their hair with Sophie-Anne's hot iron, then pulled it up with ties and clips.

"We really should do Ellen, too," Sophie-Anne says.

"What do you think, Elle?" Laurel asks. "Just a little makeup?"

"No, thanks."

"Would you do it for Meritxell?"

I stare at Madison.

"You said she was cute," Madison says. Out of the corner of my eye, Laurel reaches for her necklace. "We wear makeup for boys, so it'd probably also work for girls."

"I...um." I try to imagine myself in makeup, talking to Meritxell, but come up blank. "Okay?"

"Okay." Madison turns to Sophie-Anne. "Is your hot iron still plugged in?"

"Wait," I stammer. "I don't want—"

But Sophie-Anne is already up. She grabs a brush, while Laurel sorts through eye shadow.

Madison crosses her arms over her *Thrash 'em!* tank top and studies me. She turns for just long enough to grab a jar of foundation off the counter.

"This tone should work." She dabs a drop of beige liquid onto the side of her hand. "Tuck your hair behind your ears."

I give up and grab some clips off the counter. When my hair is pinned back from my cheeks and forehead, Madison selects a makeup brush. She leans in and begins to smooth foundation over my face. It feels strange and heavy, like a layer of paint.

"Elle," Laurel says. "Don't wrinkle your nose."

"But it feels weird."

"You'll get used to it in a second." Madison continues her work. "Now the blush, Sophie."

Blush, at least, is quick, and doesn't feel as thick on my skin. Same for eye shadow.

Then comes the liquid eyeliner.

"Look up," Madison instructs.

I tilt my head toward the ceiling.

"Just your eyes."

I jerk my head back down, fingers thrumming against my leg.

Madison sighs, and Laurel steps into view.

"Your head is shaking when you do that." Laurel splays her fingers in the air. "Madison just wants to make the lines even."

"I'm sorry."

Also nervous. The more Madison touches my face, the more I wish I could escape the bathroom. The words I use are one of the things Dr. Talia says I can control, but I keep my thoughts to myself.

Except the longer I force my body to stay still, the antsier I feel.

I focus on the ceiling as Madison draws a cold line across my bottom eyelid.

"Okay, Sophie." Madison steps back. "Hair time."

Sophie-Anne removes one of the clips in my hair, then lifts her brush.

She hits a snarl, and I wince.

"Sorry! Your hair's just so curly."

She goes through the strands slowly, carefully, but it still hurts.

Then, a hot hiss against my temple. Surprised, I jerk a little.

"Careful," Sophie-Anne says. "I don't want to burn you."

I close my eyes. As Sophie-Anne continues her work, Madison compares cosmetics brands, explaining why one is clearly superior to the others. I tune her out and try to think of Meritxell. She's who I'm supposed to be doing this for.

But every time I try to imagine her, I see Isa instead. Isa telling me I'm brave. Isa grinning when I say something they think is funny.

"All done!"

Sophie-Anne steps back. Slowly, I open my eyes.

"You look amazing," Laurel says.

"Like at least a year older." Madison nods.

I stare at myself under the harsh bathroom lights. I look like myself, but also different. My eyes seem bigger, shimmering with bronze eye shadow. My cheeks are pink and rosy, freckles completely hidden.

And my hair. At its longest in curls, it never falls below my chin. Now, it swishes against the top of my shoulders, completely straight. I tuck a strand behind my ear and it stays in place.

"Now people will notice you," Madison says. "Boys *and* girls."

I wonder if the same goes for nonbinary people, then push the thought away, hoping the makeup will conceal my flushed cheeks.

"So," Madison says. "Now that that's done, what should we do next?"

"Ellen and I started watching that cheerleading series you told us about," Laurel says.

I wait for her to explain we were also having a sleepover, just the two of us.

But Laurel swings the door to our room open wider. "Did y'all want to hang out in our room? We moved our beds together so there's plenty of space."

My body goes cold. Before I can say a word, Sophie-Anne skips into our room.

"Ooooh, I love that show!" She drops onto our combined beds. "Have you gotten to the state champs episode yet?"

We settle in. As the other girls watch the next episode, I look around at each of them. Study their hair that's perfectly straight. Their makeup that looks natural because they wear it on a daily basis. The way they finish each other's sentences.

They belong to a world I'm part of, but not.

Their words.

Expressions.

Body language.

I pick at the hem of my shorts, eyeing their dresses that pool around them on the bed. If clothes don't make you a boy or a girl, what does? Hair? Makeup? And how do you know if you're nonbinary?

Isa is so sure of themself, so confident. Then there's

me, who sometimes has trouble pinpointing what I'm even feeling.

The episode ends. Madison pauses the playlist before the next one begins. "I've seen this show a million times. Let's watch something else."

"We could find an old cheerleading championship," Sophie-Anne suggests.

"Or we could watch videos about Barcelona since we still have to catch up on"—Laurel glances at Sophie-Anne and Madison—"you know, a lot."

"Señor L isn't going to punish us for not getting all the clues right," Madison huffs. "I guarantee the school won't even let him lower our grade next year."

"I know, but he's still going to make us present something next week...." Laurel's voice gets smaller with each word. "We need time to work on that, too."

Laurel sounds how I felt right before I chickened out of reciting the second clue to Señor L. Except I wouldn't have felt like that if my team had had Señor L to ourselves. If another group of kids hadn't shown up and thrown me off.

"Emmaline and her team are already done," I blurt out.

All three of them go quiet.

"They are?" Laurel asks.

"Yes."

"Good for them," Madison says before turning back

to her friends. "While they've been focused on solving stuff, we've visited tons of places we can use for our fourth clue. It'll be easy."

"And maybe Ellen could help us on the others?" Sophie-Anne looks at me, brows rising.

I swallow hard. "We're not supposed to share answers with other teams."

"It's not like we'd tell or anything," Madison says.

"Yeah," Sophie-Anne chirps. "You wouldn't get in trouble."

"It'd really help us out, Elle," Laurel says. "Even just a tiny hint about the first clue. We've translated it, just don't know where to visit."

I think of all the time my team spent researching locations together. All the subway directions we mapped out. And now they just want me to give them the answer?

"I can't."

"Why not?" Sophie-Anne tilts her head.

My jaw aches from clenching. I already answered that. "It's. Against. The. Rules."

The pain in my jaw spreads to my neck, arms, chest. The clock *tick-tick-tick*s, as the air conditioner's hum builds to a howl.

I don't realize I've started rocking until Laurel stops me. "Calm down, Elle."

One hand on each of my shoulders. Laurel's touch

sends a painful shock through my body. I shake her off and continue to rock.

"Maybe . . . we should go."

I can't tell if it was Sophie-Anne or Madison who spoke.

"No, stay." Laurel reaches for my hands, but I ball them up tight. She can't twine her fingers through mine. "It's fine. Ellen's fine. She just gets like this sometimes."

My breath catches. Shame settles in my stomach like a heavy stone.

"It's getting late anyway." Madison slides off the bed. "Let's go, Sophie."

She disappears through the bathroom door.

"See you tomorrow, Laurel," Sophie-Anne calls back to us. "Night, Ellen."

As soon as they're gone, my breaths come easier. My fingers relax.

I wait for the sounds to lower back to a normal volume, then look over at Laurel.

"Do you want to find some Barcelona videos?"

But Laurel clicks off her iPad. "I'm just going to get ready for bed."

I get up and help her separate our beds. We move through our room like ghosts. If this were one of our stories, now would be the part right before our characters made up.

Except I can't even imagine us talking right now. Maybe the two Els can be divided and separable after all.

Chapter Twenty-Four

Day 8

Before long, Laurel falls asleep. I don't.

She sleeps with her back to me tonight. I watch her shoulders rise and fall in a perfect rhythm for what feels like hours.

Eventually, I roll over and grab my phone. 4:10 a.m. There are more group chat messages, mostly between Isa and Gibs. I scroll all the way to the most recent message but can't focus enough to read any of them.

The journey downstairs is quick, the halls dim and silent. The door is already propped open. I slip outside, then look up. The woman in the apartment across from my room must be asleep. Her windows are dark.

I make my way through the grass. Andy sits in his usual spot, but Isa is perched on my bench. The place they usually sit is occupied.

Gibs spots me first. "I thought you weren't coming."

I blink. "I thought you'd be sleeping."

Laughter. It reminds me of tapas. Port Vell.

But when I step into the light, they all go silent.

I look between them. "What?"

"It's just . . ." Andy glances from Isa to Gibs.

"You're *really* done up," Gibs says.

"You really are." Isa's voice is softer. They pat a spot on the bench next to them.

I tuck my still-straight hair behind an ear, then sit.

That's when I notice that Isa's wearing a skirt.

Flustered, I look back at Gibs. "Why are you awake?"

"Y'all've been talking up these hangouts so much," he says. "I decided I'd join one."

"Actually," Andy says, "he's just wired because he drank a gallon of Coke earlier."

Gibs shrugs. "Same diff."

I can't help stealing another look at Isa's skirt. It's purple, like their hair.

And Laurel's new dress.

Yesterday floods back to me: Breakfast. Splitting up in the subway. Overwhelm at the boquería. Xavi bailing on Andy.

"Anyhow." Andy turns to me. "You do look really nice."

The sleepover with Laurel. An unwanted makeover. My refusal to share clue answers.

My vision blurs with tears.

"I hate makeup." I swipe at my face. My knuckles come away with blush and foundation. "But I *do* like my curly hair. And freckles."

"No offense," Gibs says, "but why do you look like that, then?"

I shake my head, not wanting to talk about it. But the answer spills out.

"Laurel wanted to give herself a makeover, but Sophie-Anne and Madison showed up. Then, I was the only one not wearing makeup, and they kept asking me to let them help. I didn't want help, or any makeup, but they said it'd impress Meritxell, so—"

I swallow the rest of my words, but it's too late. I gulp air, but my breathing picks up. Faster, shallower. The garden blurs.

"Okay, am I, like, the only one here who's not gay?"

"Shut up, Gibs," Andy and Isa say together.

"Put your head between your legs." Isa turns to me. "Deep breaths."

My whole body trembles as I lean forward. I try to breathe, but—"I . . . can't."

Andy kneels in front of me. "You can. One breath in, then let it out long and slow."

Gradually, the garden stops spinning.

"Ellen, is it okay if I touch you?" Isa asks.

"... Yes."

"Okay. I'm going to put my hand on your back. Let me know if you want me to stop."

I take another breath in, then let it out slowly.

At first, Isa touches me gently. Then, more pressure as they rub soothing circles on my back, my neck, my shoulders.

Finally, I'm able to sit up.

"Sorry." Even though I feel better, my voice sounds faint and shaky.

"There's nothing to be sorry about," Isa says.

Andy and Gibs nod.

"No, there is." It's not only about the scene I just made. I suck in a shuddering breath, then try to explain. "I love patterns, like how Laurel and I are the two Els. So when I met Meritxell, I thought—I don't know—maybe it meant something. But I left you all after we agreed to see the castellers today. Andy didn't get to hang out with Xavi because of me."

"That's honestly fine," Andy says. "Xavi's cute and all, but I probably would've been super nervous if he was around."

"We had a fun day anyway," Isa says.

I definitely didn't.

"Are you sure you're okay, though?" Andy asks.

"I'll live," I say, which is true, even if it didn't

technically answer his question. I don't want to talk about my day or the scene I just made.

"Want to try to solve the third clue?" It feels like I'm grasping at anything I can reach. I glance at Isa, trying to keep my eyes off their skirt. "I didn't bring my clue sheet with me, but I could look at yours again?"

"Y'all can." Gibs yawns, then hops up from his bench. "I'm out."

"I'm getting tired, too," Andy admits. "Plus, I thought we were going to wait until next week to give ourselves a break?"

"Oh, okay." My heart sinks. It feels like I've hardly seen my teammates all day, even if it was my choice.

"We'll work on it first thing on Monday," Isa promises as we head back to the hotel together. "Want me to help you get that makeup off? I'm not sharing a bathroom, so it wouldn't wake anyone up."

Grateful for the offer, I nod.

We say goodbye to Andy and Gibs on the girls-plus-Isa floor. With every swish of Isa's skirt, my confusion builds.

"Can I ask you something?" Isa asks as they hold the door open for me.

"Yes."

"Do you really think Meritxell—or anyone—would like you more if you looked a certain way?"

They close the door with a quiet click.

"No." My shoulders round. "It's not even that. Laurel was just so excited to do makeovers. I wanted her to be happy, so I agreed."

I want us both to be happy, actually.

"She's your best friend, right? You said you're...the two Els? Something about a pattern?"

I nod as Isa grabs a tissue box off their bedside table. "Since third grade. And there's so many things on this trip with the same pattern: Meritx*ell*. Barc*el*ona. It felt like destiny, even if I don't believe in stuff like that."

Isa passes me a tissue. I blot my eyes, and it comes away with a smear of sparkly bronze.

"I don't have actual makeup wipes, but I'll do my best with what I've got. Which is basically just Kleenex, so sorry in advance."

Isa waves me into the bathroom, and I sit on the closed toilet seat. They twist the faucet on, then stick a wad of tissues under it. Soon, they're dabbing it against my cheek. My chest flutters with every cool touch while Isa's skirt sways below us.

"I don't believe in fate stuff, either." Isa's voice stays low, even though there's no one in the hotel room connected to their bathroom. "But I want to tell you something no one else here knows. Not even Andy or Gibs. Promise to keep it to yourself?"

"I promise." Isa's tissue slides toward my ear as I nod, but they don't tell me to stay still.

"Okay." Isa takes a deep breath, just like I do to steady myself. "My full first name isn't Isa, obviously. That's just a nickname. I wasn't going to share my full name with anyone because it's seriously none of their business. And this may just be a big coincidence but..."

The tissue goes still against my cheek.

"My old name was Isabel."

For a moment, I forget to breathe. Maybe I haven't given fate enough credit.

"So..." Isa's voice stays low, but it sounds different now. Vulnerable. "What do you think?"

"I think"—I tilt my head up to them, meeting their gaze for a split second—"Isa fits you much better."

"Yeah." Isa's exhale is half breath, half laugh. "No question."

"I still don't get why they put you on the girls' floor when you're not one, though."

"It could've been worse." Now that we've changed topics, Isa's words flow at their usual speed and confidence. "My parents looked at tons of schools before they found Lynnwood, all because the public schools couldn't handle my pronouns."

"That sounds like my mom and abba. Lots of schools wanted to put me in a special education program when we moved to Georgia. But I'm in advanced classes, so that's not what I needed."

"I swear." Isa shakes their head. "Sometimes adults totally freak out about labels but don't bother to get to know the person behind them at all."

Yes. That's exactly right, I think, as my attention shifts to Isa's skirt again. They turn, dropping a wad of tissues into the garbage bin.

"Can I ask you a question, too?"

"Sure, but I think we should stop asking if we can ask," Isa says. "Let's just say what we're wondering. If the other person doesn't want to answer, they don't have to. Cool?"

"Okay," I say. "If you're not a girl, why are you wearing a skirt?"

"I know some people get annoyed by this, but I'm going to answer your question with another question." Isa leans forward and wets more tissues. "What makes a skirt a 'girl thing'?"

"I don't know." Now that I stop to think about it, I honestly don't.

"So, to me, it's just another label—and not even a good one. No one complains when a Scottish guy wears a kilt, right? Because it's a Scottish thing. And when someone like Laurel wears a skirt, it's a girl thing.

"When I wear one?" Isa dabs the tissues against my other cheek. "It's an Isa thing."

That makes sense. But it leaves me with even more questions.

"Back on our first day, you said something during introductions." I search my memory. "About how there's no reason people can't use more than one set of pronouns?"

"Right. Some people do. There's a kid who uses both *he* and *they* in my therapy group."

A spark in my chest. It's hope. Maybe recognition.

"But how does that work? Does that mean they're a boy or nonbinary?"

"It means whatever they want it to mean."

"That doesn't make sense." I shake my head, and the tissue tumbles out of Isa's hand.

We reach for it at the same time and nearly bump heads. They grab it first, then toss it into the garbage.

As Isa starts on a new set of tissues, we both go quiet. My head swirls with things I thought I knew, facts that should've been irrefutable. Now it doesn't feel like I know anything for sure.

"Categories help me understand things. I make lists so everything has a place."

More silence. More dabbing.

"But I can also see why they're bad."

"Not bad," Isa says. "Sometimes they just don't tell the whole story."

I think of the game Laurel and I play, creating lives

for people based on how they look. Maybe we only ever skimmed the surface of each person but missed the bigger picture. Our assumptions could've been totally wrong.

"So you have these very specific categories," Isa says. "How do I fit into them?"

"I had to make a new list," I admit.

"Okay, I love that." Isa's grin lights up their whole face. "And honestly, labels are cool, but sometimes people need more than one to describe themselves. Sometimes pronouns change because someone's still trying to figure things out, you know? It's all good. Okay, done!"

They step away from me. My reflection stares back from the mirror, skin rubbed clean and pink, freckles visible again. My hair is still straight, but a shower will fix that.

"Thank you." I swallow a yawn.

"No big." Isa clicks off the bathroom light. "I'm glad you look like you again, mostly."

"Me too."

I follow Isa to their door.

"Buenas noches, Ellen," they whisper. "Sleep well."

I pad across the hallway.

"Buenas noches," I whisper back.

It *will* be a good night now, thanks to them.

TERCERA PISTA

¡Miren arriba, miren abajo!

Soy una gran torre de piedra

en la colina.

⁓

Viajen a pie

o en funicular,

aprendan historia,

o simplemente observen Barcelona

desde arriba.

⁓

¡Buena suerte por última vez!

Chapter Twenty-Five

Day 9

On Monday, I sit with my team at breakfast, but none of us talk. Our eyes are down, focused on our phones so no one can overhear us working on the clue.

> **Gibs (a dude)**
> My brain hurts from all these conjugations
>
> **Andy (he/him)**
> What'd I say about shafting that quiz on imperatives for basketball last semester?
>
> **Gibs (a dude)**
>

As more messages ping in, I update my pronouns in the profile settings. I study them for a moment, getting used to the new set. They feel right. And if they stop feeling that way, I tell myself I can always change them.

Isa (they/them)
I haven't figured out the location yet, but it looks
like we get to choose how to get there: 🚡
Gibs (a dude)
The other is 🕸️ 🕸️ 🕸️

I do a quick translation on my phone.

Ellen (she/her + they/them)
'a pie' means 'on foot'.

I hold my breath, waiting for someone to say something about my pronouns.

Gibs (a dude)
I am so disappointed
Gibs (a dude)
And tired. Like seriously, idk how y'all are
conscious rn

"Buenos días," Señor L calls as he enters the dining room.

I exhale. His T-shirt is blue today, with a pair of

yellow yo-yos under dialogue bubbles, each one pointing
to itself. An identical *¡Yo!* fills each bubble.

Isa (they/them)

The cable car sounds fun. Unless anyone really
wants to walk

Gibs (a dude)

Soooooo tiiiired, walking might kill me

Ellen (she/her + they/them)

I'm okay with the cable car.

Andy (he/him)

Me too, once we figure out where we're going.

Ellen (she/her + they/them)

Is Señor L's T-shirt funny because both yoyos are
pointing at themselves and saying the word for
"me" in Spanish?

Isa (they/them)

Yep!

Gibs (a dude)

Tho whether it's actually funny is up for debate

I flap my free hand under the table. The more I practice, the easier it gets to solve Señor L's T-shirts.

"Hey…"

We all look up from our phones, at Laurel.

"Hi," I manage.

This is the most we've said to each other since Saturday. She zipped out of the room yesterday morning, then I did the same thing today. No talking.

"My team is visiting Montjuïc Castle today and wondered if y'all wanted to go together." When no one says anything, she winds her purse strap around one finger. "I mean, unless you already finished clue three, like Emmaline's team."

"We were actually still working on solving it," Isa says.

All I can do is stare at Laurel. Her team wasn't even done with the first clue on Saturday, and now they're on clue three? She also just broke the rules.

"Oh." I wait for her to apologize, but she just fiddles with her purse strap. "Well, now you know. What do you think?"

"You want to work together?" Andy frowns. His gaze moves from Laurel over to Madison at the other table.

"Not really. We're positive about the location. We're just seeing if you wanted to travel together."

My phone pings.

Isa (they/them)

Andy, you cool going somewhere with M?

Andy (he/him)

Yeah, I think so...I just wish they hadn't blown the clue for us.

Me too.

Isa looks up at Laurel. "Okay, sure. That works."

"All right." Laurel releases a breath, along with her purse strap. "Let's meet after breakfast."

"Miss McKinley," Señor L calls as she's halfway between tables.

Laurel pauses.

"Can you and your team stay behind for a few minutes once you're done eating?"

"Um? Sure."

Laurel glances back to us.

"No big," Isa says. "We can wait."

I say a silent goodbye to my owl as we exit the hotel. Then Andy leads us to the subway. Gibs, Isa, and I form a barrier between him and Madison.

We transfer trains once. Except for Abba and Mrs. West, no one talks much. It feels like I'm stuck between both teams, until Laurel steps up to the same pole I'm holding to keep my balance.

"Are you mad at me?" she whispers.

Between the rule breaking and our failed sleepover, maybe I should be. But I'm honestly not sure how I feel. "I thought you were mad at me."

"Not mad. I was frustrated," Laurel admits, "but it

wasn't really your fault. I just wanted to get started on the clues so we don't get in trouble."

"You're on clue three already," I point out.

"Yeah, but..." Laurel's voice drops lower, and I strain to hear. "Only because we overheard Emmaline's team. We haven't figured out the other two clues yet."

My stomach twists. Now she's breaking rules and doing the clues completely out of order.

"Is that why Señor L wanted to talk to you after breakfast?"

"Yeah." Laurel's eyes dart to her teammates, then back to me. "We promised we'd give him a status update tonight."

When I don't say anything, she leans closer. "We already know the second clue has something to do with La Rambla. Plus, we took a ton of pictures when we went to the beach and the Olympic Village, so if the first clue is either of those, we'll be good. Once we figure that one out, we can get the next clue sheet from Señor L and pretend to do the others in the order he wants."

This sounds like a mashed-up pun from Isa's list. A cheetah who's lion to our Spanish teacher.

We get off at the next stop, then take a funicular train out of the station. It crawls up a steep hill, and the city comes into view below us.

"I thought it'd be faster," Gibs says. "Ugh, why is this so *slow*?"

I glance over at him on one side of the train car. He's like a human shield, keeping Andy out of view from Madison.

"The cable car should be better," Andy says. "We can probably even get some"—he lowers his voice—"pics of Barcelona desde arriba."

Beside me, Laurel watches them closely.

The funicular comes to a stop and we hop off, following Andy to the cable car station.

"Looks like it's up to eight people per car," he says, reading off a sign. "If we split up by team, that'd be four each, plus one adult."

Laurel turns to me. "Or you could come with us. That'd only be six in our car."

"If Ellen's going with them"—Cody steps closer to my teammates—"I'll go with you all."

"Come on, Elle." Laurel waves me toward a waiting car.

I hesitate for just a second. Laurel didn't ask what I wanted, but at least we're talking again.

Our cable cars rise, one after the other. Barcelona comes into view on one side of our car, the Mediterranean Sea on the other. Streets spread out from the beach like veins toward Plaça de Catalunya.

"Isn't it pretty?" Laurel presses her hand against the window.

"Yes." I point toward a set of familiar spires. "That's

La Sagrada Família. It's a huge church. My team went there last week."

Laurel pulls out her phone and snaps a photo, which reminds me to take out my own phone. I record the last half of the trip, panning over buildings.

Sophie-Anne joins us. "I *adore* this view."

I chew on my lip and don't say a word.

The cable car slows to a stop at the very top of the hill.

As the doors slide open to let us off, I spot the rest of my team, waiting for me.

We cross a stone bridge that overlooks a well-trimmed garden, then pay the entrance fee. I grab a free brochure as we make our way inside.

"I can't wait to see what the castle looks like." Sophie-Anne skips as she walks.

"Technically"—I look up from my brochure—"it's an old military fort."

The walls of the fortress rise on all sides of us. Up one more level, then we're out in the open, looking down at the city of Barcelona. Cody follows Andy, Isa, and Gibs as they head toward a row of cannons.

I move toward a stone ledge overlooking the Mediterranean, and Laurel follows. A pigeon watches us approach, then takes flight, a gray blur soaring toward open water.

We take everything in. Up this high, the wind whips

my hair into my eyes. I pan my phone from the sea to the docks to the beach, wondering if I can find the café we ate tapas at last week.

Nearby, Isa pulls their hair up into a ponytail. I stare at their fingers, remembering how gently they touched my face, wiping makeup away.

Isa looks up. Our eyes meet.

"The humidity is *killing* my hair." Madison steps in front of Laurel and me, fluffing her ponytail.

"Girls," Mrs. West calls. "Let's pick up the pace a little."

We climb another set of stairs and explore the top level of the fort, peeking through slits in the stone and taking pictures in front of old watchtowers. Sophie-Anne stays by Madison's side, trailing a safe distance behind Isa and the boys.

"Hey, Laurel. Take our picture?" Sophie-Anne points to a lookout area that juts out of the fort's wall, with all of Barcelona as the backdrop.

"Sure!"

Laurel snaps a couple of pics in portrait mode, then a few more with the phone turned horizontal. She hands Sophie-Anne her phone next.

"Let's get one together, Elle. Just the two of us."

My hands tingle with happiness. If we were alone, I'd flap them.

Out on the lookout spot, Laurel puts one arm around my shoulder. It prickles a little, as always, but I ignore it.

Sophie-Anne snaps our picture, studies the phone, then looks up. "This one's good! I got the whole city behind y'all."

"Does anyone want to check out the watchtower?" Laurel asks once we make it back.

"Sure," I say at the same time Madison shakes her head.

"Hard pass. I'm literally melting."

"Same here," Sophie-Anne chimes in.

I expect Laurel to agree like she's been doing all week. But then she turns to me. "Looks like it's just us, then."

If my heart had wings, it'd soar, just like that pigeon.

We stop in front of the watchtower, waiting as a woman takes a picture of two kids inside it.

"Austine, non!" the woman calls as a small girl climbs onto the fort ledge and strikes a pose, her long, white-blond hair whipping in the wind.

"What do you think, Elle?" Laurel nudges me.

"Single mom. She saved up a lot of money to surprise them with a trip to Barcelona."

"Love it." Laurel enters the watchtower as the family moves on. "And when they get home, the little girl gets discovered by a talent scout and becomes a model. Money problems solved."

The tiny watchtower is barely big enough for the two of us. As we take turns looking out over the city through the narrow stone windows, I can't help wondering about the family's real lives. Maybe the little girl isn't even a girl or doesn't like *she, her, hers* pronouns. There's no way to know.

Laurel sighs. "This is nice."

"The view?"

"Well, yeah. That's nice, too. I meant it's nice to finally be doing the scavenger hunt. I just wish we'd started sooner."

"You still have the rest of the week."

"True." Laurel moves past me, back out onto the fort's roof. "But now we'll be rushing. We don't even know what we'll be doing for our presentation."

Neither does my team, but I keep that to myself as I follow her out. We pause at a ledge that overlooks the garden by the fort's entrance.

"You really haven't figured out the first clue yet?" I ask.

She shrugs, staring down at the perfectly trimmed hedges. "Madison keeps saying the scavenger hunt doesn't matter, but...I don't know. I mean, she's been dealing with a lot between the breakup with Andy and the divorce. Obviously, she can't do anything about her parents, but Sophie and I think she and Andy need to talk. If he just explained why he's mad at her, maybe she'd be able to focus on the clues better."

This is something I hadn't considered.

Laurel sighs again, then looks around the rooftop. "We should probably go find everyone."

My thoughts race as we head toward the stairs. Maybe I can help Laurel's whole team, without breaking any rules. "He's not mad at her."

Laurel slows. "What?"

"Andy." I match her pace. "He's not angry at Madison."

"Are you sure? He seems to avoid her a whole lot."

"Yes, but only because he thinks she's upset with him for breaking up with her," I explain.

"Oh." Laurel's silent for a moment. "I think she's more confused, honestly."

We pause at the top of the stairs.

"I don't think he meant to hurt her," I say. "But he also wanted to be true to himself."

Laurel's brows scrunch. "So he likes someone else? That's why he broke up with her?"

I shake my head, just a little. "I can't talk about that. He told me not to tell anyone."

Laurel tilts her head. "But I'm not 'anyone,' Elle. We're best friends."

Yes, but . . .

"This is a secret."

"Okay." Laurel smiles. "But that's what best friends share with each other, right?"

"Right. . . ."

A group of tourists pass. When they're gone, Laurel turns back to me. "It's like when I tell you something I heard about someone at school. It's still a secret, since I only shared it with my best friend."

"Right." My voice is stronger this time. "So as long as he doesn't know I told you . . . ?"

"Yep." Laurel bobs her head. "And he won't. Promise."

"All right." I take a breath. "Andy's like me."

"Like . . . you?" Her eyes widen when it finally clicks. "*Oh.*"

I chew on the inside of my cheek. This is okay, I decide. I just won't share that it's Xavi who Andy likes.

"I never would've guessed, but that makes a ton of sense." Laurel reaches for the railing and takes a step down. "So it wasn't anything Madison did."

"No, it wasn't." I follow her down the stairs, one step after the other, until I spot our group waiting under a stone arch.

Before I can walk toward them, Laurel pulls me into a quick hug.

"Thanks, Elle."

There's a lightness in my steps as we head over to meet everyone.

Chapter Twenty-Six
Day 10

The next afternoon, my phone pings while I'm lying in my hotel room bed.

> **Isa (they/them)**
> Meet in the community room after siesta? Official
> team business
>
> **Andy (he/him)**
> Gibs is out cold. Be down as soon as I can wake him.
>
> **Ellen (she/her + they/them)**
> I'll be there.
>
> **Isa (they/them)**
> Cool! I'm already here so come whenever

I immediately get up and grab my bag, even though there's still fifteen minutes left of siesta.

From her bed, Laurel pauses the cheerleading docu-series. "Going out?"

"Just the community room. Team stuff."

"Cool." Laurel sits up. "Hey, I had lots of fun yesterday."

"Me too." First, it was the castle-fort, and then we watched YouTube videos about Barcelona culture, narrated in beginner Spanish.

"Maybe our teams can hang out again tomorrow," Laurel says. "I don't even think it'd be all that awkward for Andy and Madison, since there are plenty of other people they can talk to."

I slip on a pair of sandals. "That'd be nice."

"Yep." Laurel watches me head to the door. "Check with your team and let me know?"

"Okay. I'll ask," I promise.

Isa is alone on the couch when I get to the community room.

They look up when I enter. "Hey."

"Hi." I take a seat beside them.

The school tablet lies on the coffee table. Photos appear in neat little rows across its screen.

I point at a few that look unfamiliar. "Where are those from?"

"That was after the castellers." Isa clicks on a photo of a tall building. A small sign hangs below one of its windows.

" 'Llibertat d'opinió i d'expressió,' " I read carefully. "That's Catalan?"

"Yep. It means 'freedom of opinion and expression,' according to Google Translate. I've been doing some research. This whole region of Catalunya is part of Spain, right?"

I nod.

"But it wasn't always. It used to be separate, like its own kingdom, so some people think it should be its own country again since it has its own language, culture, and everything. Then other people who live here want to stay part of Spain."

I keep my eyes on the tablet as Isa clicks through photos. "They don't teach stuff like this in Spanish class. Or world history."

"Right? It feels like there's *so* much they leave out. Makes me wonder what they don't tell us about the history of other countries, too. Or even our own."

Before I can respond, Andy and Gibs barrel through the door.

"Sorry we're late!" Andy takes the seat across from me.

"I'm not." Gibs drops into the other chair. "I could've slept for another hour."

"I'm starting to think you might be half sloth," Andy says.

"Anyway." Isa clears their throat. "I thought we should go through photos and officially decide where to visit for the fourth clue."

"That's why you called us down here?" Gibs groans. "We've still got plenty of time."

"Three days isn't that long," Andy says.

If three days isn't long for us, it's going to be impossible for Laurel and her team to get through two more clues, plus a presentation.

"Exactly." Isa gives Andy a thumbs-up. "We should figure out where else we want to go so we can come up with a clue and create a slideshow."

"I know where we should go," Gibs says.

I don't, but I do know I promised Laurel I'd ask if her team can hang out with ours tomorrow, which gets me thinking. . . .

"Oh yeah?" Isa asks. "Where?"

"The park with the dragon-lizard statue. It was made by the same dude as La Pedrera."

Gaudí. If my team's okay with going to a park he made, maybe they'd be willing to visit another Gaudí creation.

I pull up our group chat and scroll way, way back to some of our very first messages.

"What about Casa Battló?"

The room gets so quiet, I wonder if I've accidentally interrupted someone.

"Casa what now?" Gibs asks.

"That was the other building we were looking at for clue one," Andy says. "Right, Ellen?"

"Yes." A smile tugs at the corners of my mouth. "Gaudí made both."

The room goes quiet again.

Finally, Isa turns to me. "There are just so many places in Barcelona we haven't been to yet. How come you want to go back to Passeig de Gràcia?"

"Laurel said her team had a lot of fun with us yesterday, but they're behind on figuring out their clues. I thought we could go to Casa Battló while they're at La Pedrera, then hang out together after."

"You told her where the first clue is?" Andy's voice sounds like Mom when she's practicing scales, quiet at first, then louder by the final note.

"No." I look down, wishing I could rock this tight feeling away. I squeeze my hands between my knees until an idea comes to me. "But if we go to the park first, that could give them time to figure it out. Then we could go with them and just split up when we get to Casa Battló."

"I don't know, Ellen. . . ." Isa glances at Andy and Gibs.

Desperation pools in my chest, suffocating and thick. "But we each get to choose a place to visit. That's what we decided last week."

"We didn't"—Andy clasps his hands together—"I mean, we said that there was enough time to do that, not that we were one-hundred-percent going to."

"But you went to the sports museum," I shoot back. "And if Gibs wants to go to that park, then I should get to pick a place, too."

To me, it makes sense. It's logical. Practically a rule now.

Andy opens his mouth, then closes it.

"There's an easy way to decide." Gibs sits up in his chair. "Let's vote on it."

"Vote?" Isa raises an eyebrow.

"Yeah, vote. We're a team, so we should do what the majority wants."

This *definitely* isn't what Andy said last week. My world tilts.

"I'm okay with that," Andy says.

I stare at him, but he won't look back at me.

"Same," says Isa.

Suddenly, my world's not just off-axis, it's spun itself right out of the solar system.

"Okay." Gibs leans his elbows on both knees. "Raise your hand if you want Ellen to pick a different place for us to visit on our own, without another team."

Gibs lifts his hand immediately once he's done speaking. Andy raises his hand more slowly, then Isa.

My heart sinks.

"And raise your hand if you want to go to Casa Battló and do whatever with Laurel's team before and after."

My hand is the only one that goes up.

"So that settles it." Gibs sits back. "Three against one."

"Cool." But Isa's voice is quiet again, just like after the garden, when we were talking about destiny and patterns. "Want to look through these pics and create a cover page for our presentation?"

I swallow over the thickness in my throat as Andy and Gibs make their way around to the back of the couch. I try to tell myself that this is fine. It makes sense that my teammates would want to see someplace new, not retrace our steps from the first clue.

Except, now I have to tell Laurel.

Chapter Twenty-Seven

Day 11

Or not.

No matter how many times I practiced silently to myself, the words dried up in my mouth when I tried to talk to Laurel. Because how do I tell my best friend she can't hang out with me when that's all I've wanted this entire trip?

So I'm not completely surprised the next day when Andy freezes in place on the subway train. "You can't be serious."

"Laurel?" Isa leans closer to Andy, trying to spot what he sees through the crowd of riders.

"Her whole team," Gibs chimes in.

"Maybe they're going somewhere else?" Isa says.

"Like where?" Gibs twists around the pole, then

back again. "All the other clue locations are back in the opposite direction."

The train stops to let off passengers. More people enter, the doors shut, and we're off again.

"What'd you tell Laurel yesterday, Ellen?" Isa asks.

"Nothing about the clue. I promise! I just said we were going to Park Güell today. But I didn't say they could come with us."

All true. But I also didn't say they couldn't.

"I guess there's not a ton we can do if they want to see the park, too." Andy frowns.

"Yep. . . ." Isa says. "I feel bad for Cody, though."

Me too. If I'd asked Abba to switch teams, Cody would definitely be further along on the scavenger hunt, at least.

The train stops. My teammates pretend not to see Laurel's team as we exit the station.

But no one told Abba not to talk to them.

"More intrepid travelers! What are the odds?" He makes his way toward them, forcing us to wait. Andy shoves his hands into his pockets, shoulders rounded.

"Just ignore them," Gibs tells him.

Isa nods. "We can still do our own thing."

Andy's shoulders relax a little.

Once Abba returns with the others, we head up a hill.

"This isn't as steep as Montjuïc," Isa says, "but I definitely wouldn't mind a cable car right now."

"For real," says Gibs.

I trail behind them, walking between both teams. The smack of flip-flops against sidewalk precedes Laurel pulling up beside me.

My teammates look back, too.

"We won't bother y'all, promise," Laurel says. "We're just excited to see the park."

"Cool." Gibs throws the word over his shoulder.

"So." Laurel turns to me. "I'm pretty sure I figured out the first clue last night."

I glance at her. "Oh?"

"Well, you helped me, technically."

I blink. "I did?"

"On Monday, remember?"

I do not remember.

"You showed me that church on the cable car," Laurel says. "It's literally the only thing you talked about on the ride up, so last night I realized you were giving me a hint."

I look down. If Laurel's team goes to La Sagrada Família, they'll waste another day.

As we walk past a fenced-in soccer field built into the hill, I make up my mind. I'm not allowed to share the clue location, but there's no reason I can't tell Laurel she guessed wrong.

"It's not the church."

"*What?*" I wince as Laurel's voice rises. She drops back to a whisper. "Well then where is it?"

I press my lips together.

"Come on, Elle . . . please help? I don't want to get in trouble with Señor L. We promised him we'd solve the clue today." When I stay quiet, she sighs. "Sorry. I know that's not fair to ask. Things just would've been so much easier if your dad had let you switch teams."

Guilt flares in my stomach. She's blaming Abba for something he didn't even do.

"He didn't know."

"What do you mean?" Laurel asks.

"It's not his fault I didn't switch teams. I never asked him."

"But you said . . ."

"No, I didn't." I shake my head. "I tried to explain during the group dinner, but . . ."

I trail off. My words sound flimsy.

"Seriously, Ellen?" I flinch at the sharpness in her tone. "If it was too loud or whatever, you could've told me in our room. Or literally *anytime* after."

I know. I *know*. "I didn't want to hurt your feelings."

"Well, you did. You lied, Ellen. To your best friend."

Laurel heads back to her team, leaving me alone. Stuck between two teams.

I walk in silence. I was wrong about my pun. Laurel might still be the cheetah, but I'm a lion.

"Everything all right?" I look at Isa, who's studying me.

"Careful, Mr. Gibs!" Abba calls.

Just like that, everyone's attention shifts, including Isa's.

Gibs slows down just long enough to check both ways, then sprints across the street toward a stone wall. A lizard statue stands in front, positioned like it's crawling up toward a row of colorful mosaics.

While the rest of us wait for the light to change, Gibs makes a beeline over to the statue. He turns to take a selfie. Then, movement. The statue shifts. It's not part of the wall at all, but a person in a lizard costume.

We all watch it sneak up behind Gibs. It waves as Gibs lifts his phone. Gibs yelps the moment he spots it, jumping high enough to slam-dunk a basketball.

Andy cracks up, and laughter ripples past me, all the way back to the other team.

The only people not laughing? Laurel and me.

By the time we reach Gibs, he's recovered. He snaps pics as the person in the lizard costume poses like a swimsuit model.

We buy tickets, then enter the park.

I pause as the others head toward a set of stairs that

lead to a terrace held up by stone columns. Mosaic tiles run along the top of the stone wall that circles Park Güell. Rocky stone structures rise out of the ground in every direction, accented with rainbow colors.

I take out my phone and pan it around. Recording everything, looking at nothing.

Halfway up the stairs, Gibs stops and pumps his fist in the air. "I found El Drac!"

Isa makes it to him first, and the rest of my team isn't far behind. Laurel's group snaps a quick photo, then continues the climb with Mrs. West and Abba.

"Dude, take a pic of me with my dragon-lizard buddy." Gibs passes Isa his phone.

"Dude," Isa mimics Gibs. "I'm not a dude."

They hold the camera out, then wait.

"Right, sorry."

As soon as he apologizes, Isa snaps the photo. A family stands off to one side, waiting to take their own pictures. We move so they can have their turn.

"A little closer together," the dad says in English. "I want to get the whole salamander."

Isa and Gibs glance at each other, then back at El Drac.

"Looks like we all might've been wrong." Andy laughs.

Gibs takes the next few steps two at a time, then

looks down at us. "Maybe El Drac is too epic to be just one thing. *Or* he's different things to different people."

"That is ridiculous," Isa says, "but also kind of deep."

Gibs gets to the terrace first. He disappears behind a column as the rest of us reach the top step. Above us, the ceiling shimmers with red and yellow mosaics. Cooler-colored tiles surround them in blue, green, and purple.

Gibs and Isa head toward the middle of the terrace, phones lifted over their heads. Andy wanders along the edge, where there are fewer tourists. I trail behind him, recording.

"Are you sure this is the right place?"

Madison's voice drifts over to us from the other side of a nearby column.

"Right? Like, how is there supposed to be an attic museum in a park?" That's Sophie-Anne. "Are you sure Ellen gave you the right info, Laurel?"

Andy and I both freeze.

"This has to be right," Laurel says. "Elle said the first clue wasn't at the church."

Andy whirls on me. "You told them?"

"No!"

I flinch as his arm flies up, but he points past me, to Laurel's team. "They just said you did."

Laurel appears from behind the column, then Cody and Sophie-Anne. Finally, Madison.

All staring at me.

"Ellen was just trying to help," Laurel says. "Our team is really behind."

"Whose fault is that?" Andy fires back.

Madison steps forward, hands up.

"Is it all right if I talk to Andy alone? I think I can get this straightened out." Her gaze darts to Andy, then down to her sandaled feet. "Plus, we should talk just in general, don't you think?"

Andy takes a deep breath, then lets it out. His arm lowers. He nods.

Laurel, Sophie-Anne, and Cody head back toward the stairs. I join Gibs and Isa.

"What was that all about?" Gibs asks.

"Laurel told her team that I said this is the location for the first clue. But I swear I didn't."

Isa looks past me, toward Andy and Madison. "I can't believe she lied *and* followed us here after you told her we didn't want to hang out with them."

Heat forms in my chest. It rises to my arms, my neck, my cheeks, until my body hurts. I look down at my sandals, staring at my unpainted toenails.

"Uh-ohhhh." Gibs blows a raspberry. "*Someone* didn't tell them."

Now Isa stares at me. "Is that true, Ellen?"

"I didn't tell them they could come with us. . . ." I

shift between my feet, then look up, preparing to explain myself. But Gibs and Isa aren't looking at me anymore. Their eyes are on Andy, who's speed-walking back to us.

"Let's go." His gaze bounces from Isa to Gibs to the ground. It doesn't land on me once.

"Are you all right?" Isa asks at the same time that Gibs says, "We just got here. What're we supposed to tell Mr. Katz?"

"I don't know." Andy runs a hand through his hair and tugs. "Tell him I don't feel good or it's too hot out here. Just, *something*."

That's all it takes for Isa to sprint off.

I look behind me, and my eyes lock on Laurel. She mouths something that might be *Sorry*.

It's too late now. For me, for her.

Isa returns, chest heaving. "All right, I told him. He said the three of us could stay with Mrs. West if we didn't want to leave, but I told him we all want to make sure Andy gets home okay."

Andy doesn't say a word as Abba heads toward us.

We exit the park in silence.

Abba tells jokes on the way back to the hotel. I can tell he's trying to make us laugh.

No one does.

On the subway, Andy sits beside Abba, head down. Isa, Gibs, and I hold on to a pole in the middle of the train car.

"We'll talk to Andy when we get back," Isa says. "You should've told Laurel what we decided, but she shouldn't have lied to her team. Andy'll understand."

I can't speak over the lump in my throat.

We head upstairs to the girls-plus-Isa floor. Abba waves, then disappears up one more floor.

"Hey, guys?" Isa looks at Andy and Gibs. "Can we talk for a sec?"

"There's nothing to talk about." Andy's voice is clipped.

"I think there is," Isa insists. "Because Ellen told me and Gibs that she didn't actually share anything about the clues. Laurel lied."

Lied. Lion. Lied.

I thrum my fingers against one leg as the words alternate inside my mind.

Andy takes another step away. "It doesn't matter."

"It matters to us," Isa says.

Lion. Lied. Lion. Lied.

Four more taps as Gibs nods. "She messed up by not telling them we didn't want to hang out, but she didn't share intel. Ellen's cool."

For the first time since Park Güell, Andy looks at me,

and I make myself look back as long as I can stand it. His hands grip the railing so hard, the color drains out of them. "She did share why I broke up with Madison."

My fingers freeze. I *definitely* didn't tell Madison that.

"Wait, what?" Gibs looks from Andy to me. "You seriously told Madison?"

"She told someone." Andy's voice cuts. "Because Madison knew. She told me she was 'totally supportive.'"

Each word feels like a knife aimed at my heart.

"But that's good, right?" Gibs asks. "She gets why you had to break up and isn't even mad about it."

"Ellen outed him." Isa's voice is so soft, I can barely hear it. "Andy wanted to decide when he was going to come out. Ellen took that choice away from him."

"Damn." Gibs's eyes widen with understanding.

"Yeah." Andy's voice catches. "Still think she's cool now?"

He rushes upstairs, not waiting for an answer.

Gibs glances back at Isa and me. "I'm just gonna...go."

"Text if you need anything," Isa says.

"Copy."

Then there were two.

I take a step toward Isa, but Isa holds up a hand.

"You know what you did, right?"

"I—" The rest of my words catch in my throat as Isa cuts me off.

"And why it's hard for me to trust you now?"

Pulse racing, I shake my head.

"Andy told you something private, something you promised to keep to yourself. And then you told someone else. Laurel, if I had to guess." As Isa's words flood out, my breaths get shallow, like I'm barely staying afloat. "I told you something about me, too."

"I didn't"—I try again—"I wouldn't."

"I can't know that. Not anymore." Now it's Isa who shakes their head. "I think I need some alone time, too. Later, Ellen."

Their door clicks shut, leaving me in the hall.

Chapter Twenty-Eight

Day 12

I stare into the darkness, toward Laurel's empty bed. The ache in my chest gets worse by the minute.

Laurel sat between Sophie-Anne and Madison at dinner last night, same as always. But all three kept their backs to me, while Meritxell and Xavi sat in their usual seats.

At my table, it was just me, Isa, and Gibs. No Andy. My teammates kept their eyes on their plates. No talking or texting.

Then Laurel packed her clothes, throwing all her belongings in her suitcase as I looked on. She left for Sophie-Anne and Madison's room without a word.

I roll on my side, wishing I could go back in time. I'd return to the moment before our team meeting when things started falling apart.

Or earlier. If I'd just talked to Abba last week, I wouldn't be in this mess at all.

I take a breath and let it out slowly. Over and over for what feels like hours. My mattress squeaks as I shift again. My phone screen lights up with my movement.

3:56 a.m.

What if . . .

I grab my backpack, then make my way downstairs to the garden, mentally preparing my apology. I sit on my usual bench, then pull out my diary. The last entry is from Monday night, after Laurel and I finished watching Spanish YouTube videos. While Laurel brushed her teeth and showered, I wrote about how happy we were to finally spend time together—or so I thought.

My heart twinges with every passing minute.

I've been so distracted worrying about Laurel's team's progress. Now I'm not sure how my own team is going to finish—all because I told Laurel a secret that wasn't mine to tell.

My fault. I did this.

I close my diary, unable to read through the blur of fresh tears.

A postcard slips out from between the pages.

Tomorrow we will do beautiful things, it says.

Today is technically an early tomorrow. As the

minutes tick by and no one appears, I can't see how anything will be beautiful. I'd rather look at the postcard of my owl, but it's up in my room, still pinned between my bed frame and the wall.

I stare at the hotel. Three floors up, Sophie-Anne and Madison's window is dark. I don't know what side of the building Andy and Gibs are on, but Isa's room faces the street, with all its people and pigeons and cars.

Along with the real version of my owl.

I sit up, then head for the door like someone else is in charge of my movements. I pad across the hallway, past Meritxell's room, stopping at the stairs.

My owl, my owl.

Upstairs, the postcard waits. I can look at it as much as I want.

Except, the real one is just steps away.

I move toward the front door, then stop. It's against the rules to be outside the hotel without an adult. I know this. I also know I'll feel so much better once I see my owl looking down at me.

Dr. Talia once explained that the *purpose* of rules is more important than what they literally say. I'm pretty sure the purpose of this one is to make sure kids don't go off on their own and get lost in Barcelona.

My owl is right on top of the hotel. There's no way

I'll get lost. I actually might not even need to leave the building to see it.

I pull the front door open and lean outside. But all I can see is the hotel's stone architecture, no matter how much I crane my neck.

A couple strolls hand in hand past me. My eyes track them as they cross the street, heading right for the spot where I took a pic of my owl on my first full day here.

I can't get lost, so the rule isn't saying I can't see my owl. I make my way across the street.

The owl looks down at me, its eyes a comforting yellow glow. Chin tilted up, I stare at it until my neck aches.

In just a few days, this trip will be over, I tell myself. I'll fly home and talk it all out with Dr. Talia. Every one of my decisions analyzed, dissected, so I can do better next time.

Except there won't be a next time if I've ruined all of my friendships.

I thrum my fingers against my leg, but there are no sounds to focus on to find my calm. I could rock, but I don't think it'd be enough to make this hollow feeling go away.

I try anyway.

Back and forth. Heels to toes. Arms wrapped around myself.

Eyes never leaving my owl.

It's not enough. I imagine Dr. Talia erasing the check-mark beside *Ellen's progress—Positive attitude*. I can't do anything right.

I don't immediately get jokes and puns.

Need everything organized into categories and lists.

Sometimes ask rude questions.

My owl blurs out of focus as my eyelids get heavy. I stop rocking. Coming out here hasn't solved anything.

I head back to the hotel.

A couple hours of sleep. Then I'll figure out what to do in the morning, like Abba with his drawings. He leaves his office, cleans the house, naps. Then he comes back and tackles what he got stuck on with a clear head. Maybe that would also work for friendships.

Already imagining curling up under my bedsheets, I pull on the door.

It doesn't budge.

Realization comes slowly as I stare at my hand, then the door handle. My room key can't help me down here, and Laurel has the one I need now.

I'm locked out.

Chapter Twenty-Nine

Panic lodges in my throat, tight, nauseating. My hand flies out before I can stop it. The sting vibrates up my arm, and my head clears a little. I don't smack the door again.

I take a breath, focusing on the air filling my chest.

Look around. The street is quiet. All of my overwhelm is internal.

Dr. Talia's list is about the things I can control. It can help calm me down but won't get me back into the hotel.

I pace in front of the door. There's a small button on one side of it, which could be a doorbell. I reach out to push it, then stop.

What if it's loud? It could wake up the whole hotel. Then I'd really be in trouble.

My hand drops to my side. Maybe I need to think

less like Dr. Talia and more like someone else. What would Laurel do?

All I know is Laurel wouldn't be stuck outside because she'd have the key with her. I come up empty with Andy and Gibs, too.

But Isa? They'd break this down. Take it apart and see what it's made of:

<u>What's wrong</u>: No key. Locked out.

<u>How to solve</u>: I don't know. I don't know, I don't know. This never would've happened if I'd stayed in the— Garden.

I stop pacing. Maybe there's a way to get inside from the back of the building.

Another breath. I walk the length of the hotel, from one end to the other. But if there's a garden entrance, I don't see it. Each building on this block connects to the next one.

I thrum on my leg, trying to think. Pull out my phone, check for notifications. I'm close enough to the hotel that I still have Wi-Fi, but our group chat has been silent since yesterday.

I exhale. Look up. This close to the hotel, my owl isn't visible, but light glows through the curtains on a pair of windows.

An idea starts to form. My hotel room faces the garden, but Isa's doesn't.

I click on the chat app, pulling up my direct texts with Isa. For a moment, I stare at the puns they sent me. My chest squeezes, knowing I might've ruined everything.

But I have to try. I don't want to be stuck out here all night.

Ellen (she/her + they/them)
Are you awake?

I count silently to myself, from uno to sesenta.
There's no response when I look back at my phone.

Ellen (she/her + they/them)
I'm locked outside.

There's so much more I want to say but the words are all tangled up.
My phone vibrates.

Isa (they/them)
You locked yourself in the garden?
Ellen (she/her + they/them)
No. Out front.

I wait for another message, but it doesn't come. A click, followed by the scrape of a window against its sill.

Isa pokes their head out. We look at each other for a few seconds, neither speaking.

I type out another message.

> **Ellen (she/her + they/them)**
> Hi.
> **Isa (they/them)**
> Hi
> **Ellen (she/her + they/them)**
> We don't have to talk if you don't want. I just need the front door unlocked.
> **Isa (they/them)**
> K, give me a few

They disappear.

I head back to the front of the hotel, wondering what Isa needs a few of. Seconds? Minutes? Hopefully not more. Whatever they need, I'm going to have to accept it. This isn't something I can control.

The door clicks open. I slip back inside, then turn, expecting Isa to be gone.

They stand off to one side, near the stairs.

"Thank you."

"No problem."

We both sound so polite, like we're meeting for the first time.

"I know I said I needed space, but I also know that if you don't tell me how you got stuck outside, I'll die of curiosity."

"That's not possible," I say automatically, then catch myself. "I'm sorry. You knew that."

"So . . . are you going to tell me?"

"Oh." I rock on my heels. "I wanted to see my—the owl."

"And you couldn't wait until tomorrow?"

"It was a dumb idea." I look down. "But I couldn't sleep. I understand why Andy's mad at me, and why you are, too. I needed something familiar."

Isa sighs. "I'm not mad. I just—actually, let's go back up." Isa gestures toward the stairs, and I take a few steps toward them.

"Did it help?" Isa glances at me as we walk. "Seeing your owl?"

"Maybe a little." I shrug. "But I wasn't thinking. Thank you again for saving me."

"Might as well make myself useful when I'm up this early." Isa's voice echoes, along with our footsteps. "But maybe next time—"

They freeze on the first-floor landing. It takes me a step longer to stop.

"What are you two doing up at this hour?"

Down the hall, Abba stands with the community

room door half-open, his iPad tucked under one arm. He heads toward us fast.

"More importantly, where were you coming from?"

"Nowhere, Mr. Katz," Isa says.

"You know the rules about leaving the hotel without a chaperone."

"It's my fault, Abba." I step forward. "I went outside and got locked out. Isa helped me get back in. They didn't leave the hotel at all."

"You left the hotel...." Abba looks between us. "Isa, why don't you head back to your room. I should probably talk to Ellen alone."

Isa sprints up the last flight of stairs. A door clicks open. It closes. Then, silence.

I expect Abba to lead me upstairs to his room, but he turns and gestures for me to follow.

"Let's take a walk."

I let him guide me back down the way I just came.

Together, Abba and I walk down the pedestrian avenue toward the subway. At this hour, the sidewalk is almost empty. Businesses are shuttered. There's no chirping or blurs of gray wings. Even the pigeons are still asleep.

"So." Abba clears his throat. "How'd this happen, Elle-bell?"

"I got locked out."

"Yes, I get that," Abba says. "What I'd like to know is why you left the hotel at all."

"Um. I needed..." What? To see my owl? It sounds silly now. "...some air."

"Okay. Then why not open your window?"

I swallow. That makes so much more sense than leaving the hotel.

When I don't answer, Abba leads me toward a bench just outside a playground. We sit.

"Is it all right if I..." He lifts his arm, and I nod.

Abba slides his arm across my shoulder. "I can understand not wanting to wake Laurel—"

"It's not that." I shake my head. "Laurel isn't even in our room."

"Then where is she?" Abba's voice rises. He looks around frantically, then back at me. "Did she leave the hotel, too?"

"No. She slept in Sophie-Anne and Madison's room tonight." I wrap my arms around myself. "Because I made a mistake. Actually, a lot of them."

The words tumble out. "Laurel wanted me to ask you if I could switch to her team, but I liked the team I was on, so I didn't and just let her believe you said no."

"She—what?"

I rush on. "And then she asked me to help with the

clues. Her whole team did, except for Cody. I didn't share anything, but I told her a secret about Andy, because we always used to tell each other everything and she said she wouldn't tell. But then Andy found out. Now he's mad at me and I don't know how to make things better with him, or Laurel, or anyone."

Abba rubs soothing circles on my shoulder with his thumb. "That sounds complicated, metukah."

"Very complicated." My gaze drifts across the street, to the café where Isa and I got donuts just a few days ago. But today, I don't think of custard filling or even natillas. All I can see is sandwiches behind the display counter. Jamón serrano. How hard it is to keep kosher here.

"Did you have shrimp at the group dinner? Or prawns?"

Abba's thumb goes still. "Pardon?"

"Madison said you did. She said she saw you, but I told her she was wrong."

"Honestly?" Abba sighs. "I haven't been worrying about kashrut too much on this trip. But let's keep the focus on your—"

"Why not?" Suddenly, this seems important.

"I appreciate that you're trying to look out for me, metukah. Really, I do." The stubble on Abba's cheeks lifts as he gives me a small smile. "But your ima is the more observant one."

"What are you talking about? You, and me, and Mom, we're all the same."

"We're a family, Ellen, but we're not all the same. And that's a good thing. I spent a lot of my life following the rules within a Haredi community in Jerusalem. What I wore, who I could speak to, the gender of the person I was allowed to like romantically. And yes, even the types of food I could eat."

I knew that Abba grew up in a religious community and that he met Mom when she was studying in Israel. I never thought about what took place in between.

Then I process the rest of what he said. I remember how Andy's eyes lit up when he saw the rainbow stickers on Abba's iPad.

"What do you mean about the gender of people you liked? You love Mom, don't you?"

"Yes of course. Very much," Abba says. "Sometimes identity isn't straightforward. I could have married a woman within my community, perhaps even been happy. Or maybe I could've left my community and married a man and been happy. But it was your ima I fell in love with. She knows who I am and supports me. That's what makes me happiest."

I'm not sure what to say, but Abba isn't finished.

"You practice your Judaism by following kashrut and so does your ima. Back in Georgia, I mostly do, too.

But keep in mind that no one follows the rules all the time. You eat food that isn't certified kosher. You text Laurel on Shabbat. You also handled money to pay for your donut last weekend."

This isn't something I'd thought about. It's the way things have always been for our family.

"These are choices we've made," Abba continues, "ones we've decided are right for the three of us. I'm sorry I didn't think to warn you that I wasn't going to keep strictly kosher on this trip. But I can't apologize for having a different relationship to Judaism than you or your mother do."

Despite all this new information, I feel calm. Andy and Isa also have different ways of being who they are: Andy chose to come out to a small group of people; Isa lets everyone know who they are up front.

"Do you understand, metukah?" Abba's voice pulls me from my thoughts.

"I think so." I nod. "It's why you tell your readers that any character can be shipped with anyone else in your novels: Each person's interpretation of art is unique. And you're saying that the same goes for what you believe?"

"Yes." Abba pulls me into a hug, and I hug him back. "Faith is complicated. At least, that's how I see it."

I glance back toward the hotel when we separate. "So are friendships."

My voice came out so quiet, at first I don't think Abba heard me.

But then, he chuckles. "They are, indeed. That goes for all types of relationships. But it doesn't mean they're not worth fighting for."

I agree. "I'm sorry I broke the rules."

"It's not the end of the world." Abba rises, offering me a hand. "Everyone makes a mistake at some point in their life. Usually many."

I let him help me up. My owl looks down on us as we walk back to the hotel.

"That said, I'm afraid I'm going to have to let your teacher know that you left the hotel on your own this morning. It wouldn't be fair to let this slide, just because I'm your abba."

My chest tightens a little. "I understand."

It's no fun getting in trouble, but at least I know what comes next. Abba will tell Señor L what I did, and Señor L will decide my punishment.

But facing my friends after? I can't even begin to guess the result of that one.

Chapter Thirty

An hour later, I lie in bed, thoughts swirling. I used to believe everything would make sense if I could just find a category to put it in. But I also believed Abba when he said identity isn't always straightforward, that faith and relationships can be complicated. Now, my lists seem too simple, almost pointless.

"Incoming, Ellen."

I get up and open the door.

"Ready?" Abba asks.

Something tells me it wouldn't matter what I answer. I step into the hall, where Laurel's entire team waits with Mrs. West.

I look from them to Abba, then back again before it clicks. I told Abba about Laurel asking me for clue help. Now we're all going to get in trouble.

My stomach twists. No one talks as we make our way down to the community room. No one looks at me, either.

Señor L is already waiting there by the time we arrive.

"Take a seat, everyone, please." His hands rest on his hips, giving me a full view of his T-shirt. I don't try to decode it today. "I hear you all have something to tell me."

No one says a word.

"About violating trip rules."

On the couch, Laurel's hand is at her throat, fingers tangled in her necklace. Next to her, Madison coils strands of hair around one finger while Sophie-Anne crosses and uncrosses her legs. Cody stands still as a statue behind them.

Señor L sighs. "Okay, level with me here. I can either take your version into account or make my own assumptions based on what Mr. Katz told me."

Still nothing from Laurel's team.

I take a breath. "I left the hotel without an adult this morning."

All eyes shift to me.

"I'm aware, Ellen," Señor L says. "And while I appreciate your candor, what I'd most like to know right now relates to sharing clue answers."

"We didn't share anything with anyone." Madison finally speaks up. "If Laurel asked Ellen for information, she did that on her own, without us knowing. Right, Sophie?"

Sophie-Anne freezes, leg hovering mid-cross. She presses both knees together and nods, eyes on the ground.

Laurel's cheeks flush pinker than her brightest shade of blush.

"They're right," Laurel says. "I asked Ellen for help with some of the clues because my team got stuck. But Ellen didn't tell me anything."

I stare at her, trying to figure out why she's covering for the others.

"Well, I have to say I'm very disappointed, Laurel." Señor L shakes his head. "The whole point of this trip was to discover Barcelona firsthand, an impossible goal if you aren't willing to do your own work."

"I know," Laurel whispers. "I'm sorry."

But Señor L isn't done. "Honestly, it's akin to copying homework. There's no grade associated with this trip, but I'm afraid there must still be some form of consequence."

I wince. I've never been in trouble with a teacher before. Not like this. When I was younger, I'd talk out of turn sometimes, forgetting to raise my hand before blurting out an answer. But this feels different.

"Ellen and Laurel have lost the privilege of choosing their schedule tomorrow. Both must watch the Barcelona history video I'm planning to show. It is no longer optional. Unfortunately for their teams, any remaining clue work that requires leaving the hotel tomorrow will have to be completed without them." Señor L looks from Laurel to me. "Is that understood?"

"Yes, sir," Laurel and I say together.

I look over at Laurel, but she avoids my gaze.

"All right, then." Señor L gives us a stiff nod. "Let's head to breakfast."

Once Laurel's team is gone, Señor L turns to Abba. "Thanks for bringing this to my attention, Natan. I can't imagine it was easy, what with your own daughter involved."

"Of course," Abba replies. "Ellen and I talked this through together. We'll also be having a call with her mom a little later."

I stand. "I'm sorry, Señor L. I promise it won't happen again."

"I certainly hope not." Señor L gives me a small smile. "There're only a few days left on this trip, after all."

Abba smiles, too. I don't. As far as I can tell, there's nothing to be happy about.

After breakfast, I return to my room until it's time to call Mom. My eyes trace the wall decal's curling tendrils to one end of the room, then back to its blossoming petals.

Across the room, Laurel lies curled up in bed. Her suitcase has returned, but she hasn't put any clothes back in the closet.

I miss Gibs bouncing around and Andy's laughter. Isa's patient answers to all of my questions.

More than anything, I miss what I used to share with Laurel.

My thoughts shift back to the last time I felt happy with her, up on the top level of Montjuïc Castle. I can't know for sure if she was the one who told Madison about Andy, but I also can't think of another logical explanation. "Why did you lie when you promised Andy wouldn't find out if I told you his secret?"

Laurel looks over at me. Her cheeks flush, but she doesn't say anything.

"And you lied when Señor L asked about clue sharing," I point out. "Sophie-Anne and Madison should've been punished, too."

"Things aren't always black and white, Ellen." Laurel's voice has an edge to it, but it sounds tired, a little dull. "Madison and Sophie have cheerleading camp coming up. If they'd gotten in trouble, their parents might not let them go.

And Laurel has gymnastics practice. What's the difference?

"I don't like lying, but sometimes you have to protect

your friends," Laurel continues. "At least *I* didn't lie to my best friend for no good reason."

"There *was* a reason. I liked the team I was on."

Laurel blinks. "More than spending time with me?"

"No." The word comes fast. And maybe it was true at the beginning of this trip, but now I realize it's no longer accurate. "Actually, yes."

She blinks again, eyes filling with tears.

My heart squeezes. I start to rock.

"Elle, stop."

"*No.*" I shake my head and take a breath. But I don't stop rocking. "You know this helps me, but lately it feels like you're always trying to stop me anyway. Like I embarrass you."

Tears spill down both of Laurel's cheeks. But she doesn't deny it.

"You're my best friend, but we've hardly seen each other lately," I tell her. "I thought this trip would fix things, but it didn't. I don't even think being on the same team would've helped. Not if Sophie-Anne and Madison were also on it."

The truth calms me now that it's out. I stop rocking.

Laurel sniffles, but her tears have stopped. I slide off my bed and grab a box of tissues.

She dabs her eyes as I look on. "Sophie and Madison are my friends, too, Ellen."

"I know." I hand her another tissue. "But you act different when you're around them. You want me to stop stimming. And you got quiet when I said I think some girls are cute."

"Honestly, Elle, you can like whoever you want."

I think about this. Maybe not everything is black and white, like Laurel said. Maybe she can be okay with who I like but only in private.

Except, I don't want that.

I look down at Laurel, one part of the two Els. My best-and-only friend since third grade.

"Okay." I don't want to fight about it. I don't even think I want us to go back to the way we used to be.

There's only one thing left to say. "I'm sorry I didn't tell you the truth about switching teams."

She looks up at me. "Okay."

She shakes her head when I offer another tissue, so I return to my bed. Laurel doesn't say anything else, just reaches for her phone. I reach for mine, too.

I flip through video clips, until I get to the ones from last week. Videos taken before Montjuïc, before the boquería, when things felt simpler.

I replay my first trip to La Rambla. Gibs drops coins into a street performer's cup, then we move on, toward a crowd waiting to enter the boquería. I didn't take video inside the tile shop where I bought my postcards, but I retrace every step of our journey after: glimpses of La Rambla from quieter streets and then lunch near Port Vell. My camera pans from our tapas up to the restaurant.

I pause on the rainbow-colored ad in its window, then zoom in until I can read the text. It's for an event, one that takes place tomorrow.

A series of knocks pulls me away from my phone. Laurel glances up, too, but I rise before she can move.

"It's Abba."

I head into the hall, thoughts still on my half-formed idea. It probably won't mend my friendship with Andy, but it could be a peace offering.

All I know is things won't feel right until I at least try to apologize.

Abba calls Mom on his iPad, letting me explain what happened in my own words. We agree to set up a special family session with Dr. Talia when I get home so we can work through everything as a team.

The last time we talked, Mom said teams exist so when one person needs a little extra support, the others can help them out, so this sounds like a good plan to me.

It also makes me think of Andy, Gibs, and Isa.

I steal a glance at my phone. Still no group chat messages. My chest tightens.

Mom yawns, and I look back at Abba's iPad.

"I'm sorry you had to wake up early because of me."

"Oh, it's fine. It's always nice to see your faces. Plus, it gave me a chance to check on David—look." She holds her cactus up to the screen. "I've managed to keep him alive for an entire week! Although he did prick me yesterday. Ouch, David." She frowns at him.

"Go back to bed, Miriam." Abba chuckles. "We'll talk again tomorrow, before Shabbat."

We say goodbye to Mom, then I slide off Abba's bed.

"I heard about this Basque restaurant from your teacher," Abba says. "It's near the Gothic Quarter, which we haven't had a chance to see yet, so I thought you and your teammates might want to give it a try."

"As long as they have kosher food—and vegetarian options for Isa." I look up at him. "But you can eat whatever you want, of course."

"Of course." Abba grins. "How about you go let Isa know and I'll check in on the boys. If Andy still isn't feeling great, we can always bring something back for him."

"Okay." But my chest tightens more as I head for the door. I'm the reason Andy's hiding in his room.

I head downstairs to Isa's room. A few anxious seconds after I knock, Isa sticks their head out.

"Hey."

"Hi." I tell them about Abba's lunch idea.

"Sounds cool," Isa says. "Give me a minute to grab my stuff."

They don't invite me into their room today. A reminder that I haven't been entirely forgiven.

They reappear with their bag slung over one shoulder, heading for the stairs. "Okay, ready."

"Wait."

Isa stops.

"I just wanted to say I can recite the third clue for Señor L when we get back. Andy doesn't have to be there, or you either, if you don't want."

"Thanks, but we're actually done already. Gibs texted me yesterday. We did it together right before dinner."

"Oh." I look down.

"What we really need to figure out is what to do for clue four when half of us aren't speaking to each other."

A lump forms in my throat.

"Anyway." Isa hovers by the stairwell. "Is that all, or . . . ?"

I could say yes. Then Isa and I would head downstairs, and we'd all eat an awkward lunch together.

But I don't want to spend the rest of this trip tiptoeing around each other. Not if there's a way I can fix it.

"No." I swallow, then make my way over to them. "Before I got locked out front this morning, I was in the garden. I was hoping to apologize to everyone, Andy especially."

"I don't think any of us felt like hanging out this morning, Ellen."

"That makes sense. But I want to make it up to him. And you. Or try, at least." My words tumble over one another. "Do you think you could convince him to come to the garden tomorrow?"

"I honestly don't know." My heart sinks as Isa takes a step down the stairs. "But I can ask. Meet you at our usual time, even if he says no?"

"Yes." My chest flutters just the tiniest bit. "I'll meet you no matter what."

Chapter Thirty-One

Day 13

I head downstairs at 3:55 the next morning.

The garden door is propped open, but there's no way to know if it's Isa on their own or if Andy chose to come.

My chest clenches as the benches come into view. There are two people, just like I'd hoped. But something feels off. Andy and Isa just sit there, silent and still.

Isa sees me first and waves. Andy doesn't move at all.

A deep breath, then I take a seat. "Thank you for coming."

"Sure," Isa says.

Andy keeps his eyes on the ground.

Maybe this wasn't such a good idea. If Andy really

doesn't want to see me, he might sit there and not say anything.

But I have to try. I want him to feel better so badly.

"I did an awful thing when I shared your secret with Laurel, and I'm sorry." My voice trembles.

Andy braces the bench with locked elbows.

I remember Dr. Talia's short list, the things I can control.

1. My breath: I take one, deep and full.
2. My attitude: I'll be okay, even if I can't fix all of my friendships.
3. Then there are the words I use.

"Friendships are hard for me. It feels like there are so many rules and they don't always stay the same. I've only ever had one friend before this trip, and now Laurel and I both have a new group," I continue. "But I kept trying to make us work like we used to. For me, that meant telling her a secret that wasn't mine to share."

"Yeah, it definitely wasn't." Andy's words cut through the air between us.

I glance over at Isa, who gives me a quick thumbs-up. I make myself go on.

"I'm sorry. I know it's too late to take back what I

shared, and I know you don't have to forgive me. But I had to try because this feels like the first time since Laurel that people really like me for me. It's almost like we're—"

"Friends?" Andy tilts his head, voice softer.

I swallow hard. Nod.

"Duh." Isa shrugs when Andy and I look at them. "I figured I'd fill in for Gibs."

Out of the corner of my eye, I catch Andy smile. It's nothing like his wide grin at Port Vell, but it's something.

The smile is gone when he turns back to me. "You know why I'm mad, right?"

Another nod. "I took away your choice to decide when to come out to other people."

"Yeah."

"I understand if you don't forgive me," I go on. "But I still wanted you to know I'm sorry. Plus, there's another reason I asked to meet up this morning."

"I'm listening."

"Do you know what Pride Month is?" I ask.

"Yeah," Andy says. "I mean, kind of. It's to celebrate boys who like boys and girls who like girls, right?"

"And people like me," Isa chimes in.

And dads like Abba. And Ellens like me.

I pull out my phone and click to the screenshot I took by Port Vell over a week ago.

"There's going to be a parade later today." I show

Andy and Isa the rainbow-colored poster. "I have to stay at the hotel to watch Señor L's movie, but I thought you might want to go."

"...With your dad?" Andy asks.

"Yes. He wouldn't even ask why you want to attend, either, I bet."

"No bet," Isa says. "Mr. Katz is cool."

"I'll think about it." Andy stands. He says goodbye, then heads back inside.

"How do you feel?" Isa asks.

"I don't know." I allow myself to rock a little. "But I said what I needed to."

"Yep." They push up from their bench. "That's all you can do."

We head inside together.

"If we do go to the parade," Isa says, "we'll figure out our presentation when we get back, okay?"

They hold the door open for me.

"Or..." I'm the only one who hasn't recited anything for Señor L yet, but my stomach twists just thinking about this. "...I could work on it while you're at the parade. If you go, I mean."

"That's cool," Isa says. "How about you text us your ideas this morning and we'll figure it out together at breakfast?"

I step inside, and they click the door shut behind us.

"Okay." That's something I can do—at least, after a little more sleep.

At breakfast, I join my team at their table and Laurel joins hers. My heart still twinges a little when I see her, but my axis doesn't tilt.

Gibs salutes me as I sit down beside Isa. Andy nods, then looks down. We focus on eating as our classmates chat around us. A current of excitement ripples from one table to the other.

"—think you know where we're going for Saturday's dinner?"

"Could be a museum. Another castle?"

"What about that big Ferris wheel up in the hills?"

"So." Gibs finally breaks the silence. "Are we just gonna stay inside all day again, or . . . ?"

"I'm kind of tired of our room, to be honest." Andy twists his paper napkin. "Ellen had an idea that I think would be kind of cool. If others want to go, I mean."

"Ellen had an idea," Gibs repeats. "And she told you about it when, exactly?"

"This morning," Isa says. "You were sleeping, as usual."

For once, Gibs ignores Isa. He looks from me over to Andy. "So y'all've made up now?"

Andy shrugs, then twists up his napkin. It's not the yes I'd hoped for, but it's also not a no. "There's a parade happening for Pride Month," he says. "That's for people who—"

"I know what Pride is," Gibs interrupts. "I'm not dumb."

Isa snorts.

"Usually, anyhow."

"You don't have to come if you don't want," Andy says. His napkin's so tightly coiled, it looks like a paper snake, thin and long.

"Of course I'm going." Gibs spears the last piece of jamón on his plate. "If y'all are coming, so am I. Besides, you couldn't pay me to sit through Señor L's—"

Isa shakes their head, and he stumbles to a stop. "Sorry, Ellen. The movie won't be that bad. Probably."

"It's fine." I honestly mean it. "Parades are loud and crowded. I won't need headphones for the movie."

Plus, I want Andy to enjoy the day, not worry that I'll tell people things he doesn't want me to share.

"You're okay with going to the parade, too?" Andy asks Isa.

"Totally okay," Isa says. "I thought it was a cool idea the moment Ellen mentioned it."

Andy releases his napkin, hands relaxing.

"I also had an idea for our fourth clue," I say. "I know we could just do Park Güell, but we weren't there very long, and I don't think it's a good memory for anyone."

"Except for meeting my lizard-dragon-salamander friend," Gibs says.

Emmaline glances over, and my phone pings a second later.

Isa (they/them)

Maybe tell us on here so we can brainstorm in

private?

For the rest of breakfast, we trade ideas in our group chat, until it feels like we have a solid plan. When our classmates start to head out, Andy stands. "Let's go ask Mr. Katz about the parade."

"Bye, Ellen." Isa waves.

I wave back. "Have fun."

Across the room, Laurel stands alone, her teammates already gone. She glances at me, then looks away, one hand on her cross charm.

I head over. She's wearing a lacy shirt I've never seen before. "Is that new?"

"Yeah. I got it last week when my team went shopping. Do you like it?"

I imagine the scratchy lace against my skin, how the

wide, scooped collar would probably slip off my shoulders. I'd have to slide it back into place, over and over.

"I think it's perfect for you."

Laurel smiles, just a little.

"Ready for the movie?" I ask.

"I guess." She shrugs. "It's not like we have a choice, right?"

"Correct." I wave her toward the door. "Let's go together."

"All right, y'all." Señor L shuts off the projector and flips the lights back on. "Any questions?"

Laurel and I shake our heads.

"Just one, actually." Emmaline makes her way up to him, brandishing a pen and notepad.

Beside me, Laurel looks down at her phone. "My team is dropping by to pick me up in a minute," she says. "See you later?"

Part of me wants to know if they ever figured out the first clue. I remind myself that some things are out of scope. I don't need to know.

"See you later."

Emmaline skips past us and Laurel follows. I sink back into a chair.

"Ellen?"

I look up at Señor L, who's rolling up his projector screen.

"Did you want to talk about the movie?"

I shake my head, but start talking anyway. "It was interesting," I say. "Like, I didn't know some people speak Catalan before this trip. We haven't talked about it in class."

"That's a very good point. Perhaps I can incorporate some of this into my lessons next year." He goes on, "And despite the unfortunate clue sharing business, I hope you've enjoyed your time in Spain, Ellen."

"I have."

"Fantastic." Señor L tucks the projector under one arm and his laptop under the other. "Enjoy the rest of your day."

Alone in the community room, I remember my first morning when I woke up early and called Mom. I watched my first video of Barcelona here, too, plus met my new teammates. So much has happened since then, things I haven't written down in my dot diary yet.

I head out. Clicking the door shut, I turn, right as Meritxell, Xavi, and their parents appear.

Xavi and the grown-ups pass me on their way to the dining room, but Meritxell slows.

"Bona tarda, Ellen."

"Hola, Meritxell," I say back. "¿Cómo estás?"

"Bien," she says. "Your pronunciation is better."

"¿Ah, sí?"

"Yes," she confirms. "When do you leave?"

"Our flight leaves on Sunday morning," I answer in Spanish.

Meritxell smiles. "¿Has disfrutado este viaje?"

"Sí." I continue in Spanish. "I enjoyed Barcelona, and it was nice to meet you. Also Xavi."

"Nice to meet you, too. Adéu." She disappears into the dining room.

It's not until I'm back in my room that I realize I had a conversation with Meritxell, completely in Spanish. Maybe I can handle presenting the fourth clue after all.

I settle onto my bed with my dot diary. The last time I wrote down my thoughts was Monday, but the entry was more about Laurel than Montjuïc Castle. I begin to fill in the blanks, leaving nothing out, from our team meeting on Tuesday to the trip to Park Güell. These aren't the happiest memories, but I record them all.

I'm not sure how much time has passed when my phone vibrates. Still lost in thought, my pen hovers above my diary as I check my notifications.

It's Abba.

Kind of.

Abba

Hi, Ellen. Isa here. Your dad's letting us use his phone so we can talk to you while we're out.

Abba

Andy says hi too.

Abba

It's so humid out here it feels like a sauna punched us 🥵 👊🏿

Abba

That was Gibs 🙄 And this is Isa again (confused yet?).

A smile tugs at the corners of my mouth.

Ellen Katz

Hi. What's the parade like?

Instead of another text, my phone buzzes with a video request. I click accept, and I'm treated to half of Isa's face, half of Gibs's.

"Hey!" Isa raises their voice over the background noise. "The parade is awesome."

I turn the sound down. Now it's not too loud but not so quiet that I can't hear them.

"Yeah, it's—" Gibs says a word that's either "fun" or "dumb." I think I can guess which one from his smile.

The phone changes hands, and Andy comes into view.

"It's super loud here," he says. "But also awesome."

"So awesome." Isa takes the phone back. "And we wanted to share it with you."

The screen shakes as they turn the phone away from their face.

So many people. Milling around. Walking, talking, and eating food on the sidewalks. Some have their faces painted and others hold rainbow flags. There are other flags, too, in almost every primary, secondary, and tertiary color.

In the quiet of my room, I don't have to hit record and return to it later. I sit back and watch everything as it's happening, at a volume that's manageable for me.

Boys hold hands with other boys, same for girls with girls. Sometimes I can't figure out if I'm looking at someone who's a boy, a girl, or some other gender. That's okay. There's room to add categories in my dot diary for all types of people—and also for myself.

The crowd starts clapping as one. Isa lifts their arm so I can see over people's heads, to the street where a float rolls past. People's heads bob at the bottom of the screen, all dancing.

Isa passes the phone to Gibs, then Andy, and finally Abba, who lifts it high enough for me to see rows of acrobats tumbling down the street. Each person wears one color of the rainbow flag, their movements perfectly in sync.

It feels like a holiday. A celebration of every identity. Each unique set of pronouns, maybe more than one set for some people.

Eventually, Abba lowers the phone and turns it around. "I want to save as much phone battery as I can while we're out and about. I'm afraid we'll have to say goodbye, Elle-bell."

He pans the camera to Andy, Gibs, and Isa. They all wave to me.

"Happy Pride, Ellen," Isa yells.

"Happy Pride." I wave back, both hands flapping.

And I mean it. Especially the happy part.

Chapter Thirty-Two

Day 14

On Saturday, Señor L leads us to the metro. A few stops later, we hop off the train at a station that puts us at the end of La Rambla, near Port Vell. We cross the street, and the Mediterranean Sea comes into view, each wave a ripple of deep blue in the evening sunset.

In front of my team, Clara turns to Emmaline. "We must be eating on the beach!"

But Emmaline shakes her head. "There'd be nowhere to plug in Señor L's projector."

"Maybe a restaurant near the water?" Clara tries again.

I glance at Isa. "Where do you think we're going?"

"Honestly? I don't really care as long as we get to hang out together."

I can't tell if the "we" means our team or just Isa and me. My cheeks can't tell, either, but they heat up like it's the second option.

Señor L doesn't enter any of the restaurants when we get to the boardwalk. He leads us onto a dock.

"We're having dinner on a boat?" Gibs asks. "This actually is gonna be cool."

"Yes, Mr. Gibson," Señor L calls over his shoulder, "occasionally teachers are cool."

We file onto a bright blue boat, into a room set up with tables and chairs. Glass windows look out onto a deck that wraps around the entire ship.

Señor L sets up his projector screen at the front of the room.

"Drop your tablets up here," he says, "then siéntense, todos, por favor."

Isa follows Emmaline, Tess, and Cody to the front with our group tablet, then returns to the tables. Señor L didn't say that we had to sit with our teams, but everyone does, except Cody, who sits beside Jake.

As servers pour us water, Señor L moves to the front table.

"Enhorabuena. You survived Barcelona, as far as I can tell." He chuckles. "Tonight's presentations serve as the capstone for this trip. I look forward to trying to figure out each of the clues y'all came up with."

Isa nudges me, and a current of nerves shoots through my body.

"El primer equipo: Clara, Emmaline, Peter, Daniel, and Jake."

They present their clue in Spanish, then we all throw out guesses.

The longer it takes to find the answer, the louder the room gets as kids laugh, clap, and sometimes clang silverware.

I thrum my fingers under the table, focusing on what I can control. A deep breath in, then a long, calming exhale.

"El siguiente equipo," Señor L calls. "Andy, Noah-James, Ellen, and Isa."

Isa turns to me. "Are you ready?"

I nod as Andy sprints over and plugs in our tablet. Isa and Gibs stand on either side of me, looking out at our classmates.

The screen bathes us in artificial light. Our collage is a blend of the locations we visited on our scavenger hunt, plus other places: La Sagrada Família and Park Güell. The subway near our hotel. The donut café.

Plus us: Gibs stuffing his face with a custard-filled donut. Andy in an FC Barcelona jersey he bought at the sports museum. Isa waving a tiny flag with yellow, white, purple, and black stripes. Abba's drawing of us on the subway.

And my favorite: our shadow-selves waving at real-us on the roof at La Pedrera.

I spot Abba with the other chaperones. He leans back in his chair. Sends me a smile.

The screen goes dark, then lights up again, as a recording plays over the speakers.

My voice, in Spanish.

Yo nunca duermo,
ni por la noche.
Yo nunca como,
aunque hay tapas y paella en mis restaurantes.

I glance back. Shortened clips of my videos match the recorded words. Isa's handiwork.

Encima de mí, un castillo.
Debajo de mí, un puerto con barcos.
En todas partes hay diseños de un famoso
arquitecto llamado Gaudí.

My pronunciation isn't perfect; *r*'s aren't always rolled.

None of that matters because my teammates helped me come up with this clue. We chose it together.

Then, it's over. The room fills with classmates translating and guessing.

"I don't sleep—"

"—don't eat."

"Whose restaurants are filled with tapas and paella?"

I focus on Emmaline and her team, seated at the table closest to us.

"I think the second part's about the clues we solved. . . ." Jake says.

He scrunches his eyebrows at the same moment that Emmaline's eyes widen. "Barcelona?"

She aims the question at Gibs.

"What about it?" he asks, but the corners of his mouth quiver, like he's holding back a smile.

"The answer," Emmaline says. "It's the city of Barcelona. All of it, right?"

Gibs gives her a small nod.

"*Such* a cool idea!"

The tips of his ears flush pink.

"It was indeed." Señor L claps, and the others join in.

We return to our seats as Señor L calls up the next team, then finally Laurel's. Their presentation is a series of pictures that look like they came from Google, their clue about Park Güell. Once we've solved it, it's time for dinner.

Tapas fill trays on each table. I spot the patatas bravas and take a big serving.

At the adult table, Abba fills his plate, too. I can't help trying to spot what he's chosen. He catches me looking, and I hold his gaze, just long enough to let him know

I'm okay. With whatever he's going to eat. With how this whole trip turned out. Everything.

Everyone talks and eats and laughs while I soak it all in. My body starts to feel heavy, like it did after we got back from La Sagrada Família. I slip on my headphones and the noise blissfully lowers. No one tells me I'm being rude.

Soon, the servers clear away our plates, and we're allowed to explore other parts of the ship. I make a beeline for the nearest exit, stopping only when Señor L holds up a hand.

"Just one final announcement. Actually, more of a reminder. Don't forget to check in for our flight when we get back to the hotel tonight if you haven't already. Beyond that, no horsing around on the deck," he calls as kids stream out of the room. "I don't want to spend my last night in this beautiful city fishing kids out of the sea."

Outside, the air is hot and humid, but a salty breeze cuts through it. The last hint of light glimmers far out on the water as I find a quiet spot away from my classmates. I hold the rail and rock a little, my head back, letting the wind whip my curls.

"Hey, Elle?"

"Hi." I turn toward Laurel. Her necklace glints under one of the ship's lights.

"Your clue was really cool. It was also pretty awesome

how Tess's team used a person instead of a location for their clue."

I nod. "If Señor L hadn't given up on that one, we'd probably still be guessing."

"Yeah." She bites her lip. "So, I was wondering . . . did you want to check in when we get back to our room? So we can get seats together on the plane again?"

She fidgets as I take a moment to think through both questions. I should be thrilled that she's asking me to sit with her.

But I have a feeling we would both like to sit with different people tomorrow. At the start of our trip, this would have bothered me. Not anymore. Not now.

"We sat together on the way here. I think you should sit with Sophie-Anne and Madison on the way back."

She goes still. "Are you sure?"

"Yes."

"Okay." She pulls me into a quick hug. "Thanks, Elle."

Then she's gone, off to find her new friends, if I had to bet. Farther up the deck, Isa stands at the railing beside Andy and Gibs, looking out at the sea.

Call it destiny, or a pattern. The exact word doesn't matter. I know where I'm meant to be.

I sprint down the deck to join my team.

Chapter Thirty-Three

Beautiful Tomorrow

My alarm vibrates me awake on our final day in Barcelona.

I slip into my comfiest clothes but pause when I reach the door. It's not Laurel I'm looking back on this morning, although she's here in the room with me, in her usual deep sleep. Wedged between my bed and the wall, my owl postcard looks back at me.

I grab it.

Isa is alone when I reach the garden.

They turn. Smile. "There you are."

"Here I am."

"Andy's having some issues waking Gibs." Isa holds up their phone. "I told him we'd come up and help."

I glance at my phone. There are no new notifications, but maybe Andy messaged Isa on a different chain. "Okay."

Both boys are waiting for us in the third-floor hall.

Gibs sits cross-legged on the floor while Andy leans against a wall.

"Finally!" Gibs hops up. He climbs halfway up to the next floor, then stops. "Well, come on."

"He's either going to be hyper the entire flight or passed out," Andy tells us. "You two are lucky you get to sit with Mr. Katz."

I study my friends. Something seems off. It doesn't look like Gibs has slept yet at all.

But Andy and Isa are already climbing the stairs, following Gibs.

One floor up, my questions continue to build. "Where are we going?"

"It's a surprise," Gibs calls. His voice echoes down the hall.

Isa and Andy shush him.

"Do you trust us?" Isa asks.

"Yes."

"Then no more questions," Andy says. "You'll see in a second."

I don't like surprises, or changes to plans, or last-minute detours. But I follow them up one flight of stairs, then another.

The stairs end on the sixth-floor-that's-really-the-seventh, where the ceilings slope lower. Andy heads to a door that looks exactly like the one to our garden.

"Ellen first." Gibs bows like a butler.

Cool night air tickles my face as I climb onto the hotel's roof. "Should we be out here?"

"It's not breaking any rules," Andy says.

"Yeah." Isa smiles. "We haven't left the hotel."

I look between them. "How did you even know we could get up here?"

"You can thank Andy for that," Gibs says. Leaves crunch under his feet as he makes his way to the ledge and peeks over. "Y'all should really come look."

Isa offers me a hand. I take it, and every concern vanishes.

Andy walks next to us. "Xavi told me he and Meritxell used to come and play up here each visit when they were younger. Gibs and I ran into him last night after we got back from the boat dinner."

I let Isa guide me toward Gibs, then go still as I step underneath a familiar shadow.

"My owl..."

It's just a couple of metal supports from the back. Nothing special. But I can still make out the shape I know so well. I settle into a place on the ledge between Andy and Isa.

"It's obviously cooler-looking from the front," Isa says, "but how many people can say they've been this close other than us?"

I don't answer. Isa squeezes my hand and I squeeze back.

There's something I still need to do. I look out over the ledge, trying to build up my courage. We're not high enough to see the sea, and it's too dark to spot La Rambla.

"I have something for you all."

Three pairs of eyes fall on me as I pull the postcard out of my bag.

Gibs takes it first and shows it to Andy, who passes it to Isa.

"I'm sorry I only have one," I say as Isa studies the front, then flips it backward.

They look over at the boys. "Did y'all see what Ellen wrote on the back?"

"No." Andy shakes his head at the same time that Gibs says, "Did you just say 'y'all'?"

Isa passes the card back to Andy. "Thought I'd try it out now that I live in the South."

Andy skims the card, then grins.

"'Owl I need is you,'" Gibs reads over Andy's shoulder. He laughs. "Ellen made a pun!"

"Yeah they did," Isa says. "An awesome one."

Warmth floods my chest.

Then I process what Isa said. "You called me 'they.'"

"You changed it in the group chat, so I figured I'd try it out." Isa studies me. "Is that okay?"

"Yes." Slowly, I nod. "You can use either set."

The city spreads out as I glance over the ledge again. I miss Mom and my own comfy bed, but Barcelona feels like a second home now. I take in the twinkling lights and savor the quiet—

—until Gibs breaks it.

"I still can't believe y'all woke up at the crack of dawn every morning for two straight weeks."

I blink the sparkles out of my eyes and spot Andy's and Isa's matching grins. Like laughter, it's contagious. My expression matches theirs.

"And I can't believe it's the end of June." Andy sighs. "Summer's almost half over already."

"Got any plans for the rest of it?" Isa asks.

"Basketball camp." Gibs mimics a shot.

Andy nods. "Same here."

"And I've got lots of unpacking in my future," Isa says. "Probably babysitting and watching Disney movies, too."

"What about you, Ellen?" They turn to me.

I think of Laurel and all the sleepovers that probably aren't going to happen now. I think of my teammates and how there's no way to know if we'll stay close once school starts. Andy and Gibs are popular athletes. Isa could make friends with anyone.

The first sliver of sunrise spills over rooftops in front of us.

Tomorrow we will do beautiful things, Gaudí said. That quote used to make me anxious.

But not every person fits neatly into categories. Life doesn't always stick to a planned itinerary.

Right now, it's enough to watch the sun rise with my friends.

"I don't know yet," I admit. "I think I'll just take it one day at a time."

✤ ✤ ✤

AUTHOR'S NOTE

Middle school was tough for me. While I got good grades, I struggled to connect with my classmates socially. Like Ellen, I had a best-and-only friend, a classmate who didn't seem fazed by what made me different.

This friend was a lifeline at school, someone who helped me navigate confusing social rules that my classmates naturally understood. And when we were alone, we watched movies, talked about our favorite book series, and had many fun sleepovers.

Then my family relocated from Minnesota to Georgia, and I had to start over. My new school felt like a foreign country where I didn't speak the language. Without my best-and-only friend, I had no one to help me fit in.

In reality, my relationship with my friend had started to change long before my family moved away. Over the years, her circle of friends expanded. Although she continued to include me, I struggled to understand how I fit into her new, more complex social life.

My interests changed, too. As figure skating became increasingly important to me, I saw my friend less and less.

It wasn't until years after I finished school that I learned I am autistic. Suddenly, my struggles to fit in and my hypersensitivity to sensory input like lights, noise, and touch made sense.

Autism is known as a "spectrum" condition because there is a wide variety of challenges that autistic people may experience, such as innate difficulties understanding the way neurotypical individuals socially interact and communicate, and hyper- or hyposensitivity to sensory input. Some autistic individuals engage in repetitive behaviors like rocking and hand flapping to manage or express their emotions. Autistic people can be verbal, or nonverbal. Some nonverbal autistic individuals communicate in writing or by other methods. Ellen's experiences with autism are unique to her and not intended to be viewed as the only autistic experience.

Like Ellen (and myself), many autistic people find comfort in set schedules. Even slight changes to a routine can be distressing and make our world feel like it is spinning off-axis. Canceled plans or last-minute changes can be very stressful.

They're also a part of life.

My family's relocation forced me to adjust and make new friends, just like Ellen's class trip required that she get to know other classmates. Without my best friend around to be my guide, I had to learn to navigate on my own. I stumbled at first. Made mistakes. But eventually, like Ellen, I found friends who accepted me.

If you have questions or would like more information about what it's like to be autistic, I encourage you to check out some wonderful, reputable online resources like Autistic Self Advocacy Network (ASAN—autisticadvocacy.org), Autistic Women & Nonbinary Network (AWN—awnnetwork.org), and Identity-First Autistic (identityfirstautistic.org). Reading and researching other narratives—novels, nonfiction, and blogs—can also be a great way to understand and empathize with the autistic community.

✤ ✤ ✤

ACKNOWLEDGMENTS

Your second book is going to be hard. I've heard this expressed by so many authors. So, when I sat down to write the first draft of *Ellen Outside the Lines*, I assumed it'd be a challenge—and it absolutely was.

That's why I'm grateful for the people who read Ellen's story early on and urged me to keep writing. Thank you to my agent, Jordan Hamessley, for your feedback and encouragement from the earliest stages of this story's development. I couldn't do this without your guidance or the support of the other wonderful folks at New Leaf Literary.

My editor, Lisa Yoskowitz, expressed enthusiasm for Ellen's story when it was little more than a synopsis and a handful of chapters. Lisa, your insightful observations and feedback helped me elevate this story and shape it into something I will always be proud of—todah rabah.

Ellen's beautiful, vibrant cover wouldn't exist

without the masterful work of cover artist Ana Hinojosa and cover designer Angelie Yap. Thank you both for bringing Ellen and Barcelona to life in such vivid detail. Thank you as well to my amazing publicists—Katharine McAnarney and Marisa Russell—to Hannah Milton as assistant editor, to production editor Marisa Finkelstein, copy editor Vivian Kirklin, the marketing team of Stefanie Hoffman, Shanese Mullins, Mara Brashem, and Christie Michel, and the rest of the Little, Brown Books for Young Readers team who helped bring Ellen's story to readers.

So many people took time out of their lives to read parts of this manuscript. A special thank-you to Nicole Melleby for all the support and feedback (and text messages!). I'm grateful for your notes, of course, but I'm even more grateful for our friendship. Thanks also to Joy Ding for being one of my longest and staunchest writing friends. I am beyond fortunate to know you!

Thank you, Julie Artz, Eric Bell, Jennifer L. Brown, Katrina Emmel, Maria Frazer, Sarah Kapit, Hannah Kates, and Jessica Vitalis for your notes on early chapters and on my synopsis. To Sandra Proudman for your feedback on my entire manuscript and insight into Mexican American culture and the Spanish language. Thank you, Ellen Melleby, for your notes on the Spanish language used by my American characters. And a big muchas gracias to

Alena Pons for helping ensure the Castilian and Catalan phrases used in this manuscript are accurate, as well as organic to the characters speaking them.

Virtual writing groups were the only reason I got anything done while sheltering in place at home in 2020 and 2021. Thanks for keeping me consistently writing, Camille Baumann-Jaeger, Alex Brown, Mary Chadd, J. Elle, Sharae Green, Jennifer Honeybourn, Mallory Lass, Gina Loveless, Karen McCoy, Taj McCoy, Anna-Marie McLemore, Lee O'Brien, Jamie Pacton, K Lynn Patterson, Justine Pucella Winans, Sandra Proudman, Mary E. Roach, Laura E. Southern, Shannon A. Thompson, and Taylor Tracy.

My parents, Vicky and David Sass, encouraged my love of language-learning and travel from the very start. I still cherish the books you brought me back as gifts from your business trips, Dad. And Mom, you've always supported my voracious love of languages, never telling me that trying to learn three at a time (or four, or five...) was too much. This book exists because you both encouraged me to follow my interests.

To my brother Michael, my sister-in-law Cathryn, and nieflings Peter, Daniel, and Clara: I love you and wish you many exciting adventures in the years to come.

I would not be able to put the necessary time and effort into my work as an author without the support of

Deven Cao

A. J. Sass

(he/they) is the author of *Ana on the Edge* and *Ellen Outside the Lines*. He is an avid traveler who loves learning about different languages and cultures. After five business-related trips to Barcelona, he was thrilled to finally return as a tourist to do research for this book (which involved Gaudí tile-spotting, mastering the subway, and eating a custard-filled donut for breakfast each morning). When he's not experiencing new places, A. J. lives in the San Francisco Bay Area with his boyfriend and two cats who act like dogs. He invites you to visit him online at sassinsf.com.

my boyfriend, Deven Cao. He also reminds me to take breaks, to savor what I've already accomplished, and to keep looking forward. Thank you, Deven, for being the most wonderful partner.

Lastly, thank you to every person who has read *Ana on the Edge* and *Ellen Outside the Lines*, and thank you to the bloggers, parents, librarians, and educators who have ensured my stories get into readers' hands. Your efforts and enthusiasm are so appreciated.